Welcome!

Dear Reader,

Welcome to a world of imagination!

My First Story was designed for 5-7 year-olds as an introduction to creative writing and to promote an enjoyment of reading and writing from an early age.

The simple, fun storyboards give even the youngest and most reluctant writers the chance to become interested in literacy by giving them a framework within which to shape their ideas. Pupils could also choose to write without the storyboards, allowing older children to let their creativity flow as much as possible, encouraging the use of imagination and descriptive language.

We believe that seeing their work in print will inspire a love of reading and writing and give these young writers the confidence to develop their skills in the future.

There is nothing like the imagination of children, and this is reflected in the creativity and individuality of the stories in this anthology. I hope you'll enjoy reading their first stories as much as we have.

Jenni Bannister

Editorial Manager

Imagine...

Each child was given the beginning of a story and then chose one of five storyboards, using the pictures and their imagination to complete the tale. You can view the storyboards at the end of this book.

The Beginning...

One night Ellie was woken by a tapping at her window.

It was Spencer the elf! 'Would you like to go on an adventure?' he asked.

They flew above the rooftops. Soon they had arrived...

Derbyshire & Nottinghamshire Tales

Contents

Mellers Primary School, Nottingham

Ruby Richardson (6)	67
Omar Nyandou (6)	68
Joshua Rozee (6)	70
Hamza Mehmood (6)	71
Nevaeh Regan-Turner (6)	72
Diwan Sherif (6)	73
Jasmine Sobiesinska (6)	74
Yasmin Elayeb (6)	75
Halima Jammeh (5)	76
Aween Fatah (6)	77
Nour Zurqani (5)	78
Ahmed Salama (6)	79
Fahim Ali (6)	80
Mohammed Abodhir (6)	81
Binta Danso (6)	82
Mohammed Abdulkadir Abakir (6)	83
Elyas Al-Jalam (6)	84

Scarcliffe Primary School, Chesterfield

Oscar Daniel Gilliver (7)	85
Lewis James Tye (7)	86
Ethan Richard Bytheway (7)	87
Oliver Raben (6)	88
Scarlett Smyth (6)	89
Logan Andrew Webb (7)	90
Katie Allen (6)	91
Isabella Hyslop (6)	92
Hope Lily-May Webb (6)	93
Harry McEwan (6)	94
Joshua Clarke (7)	95
Ebony Jade Cauldewell (6)	96

Shirland Primary School, Alfreton

Darcie Jones (7)	97
Lexi Wilkinson (5)	98
Aimee Louise Hingley (6)	99
Ellie Grace Hodgetts (7)	100
Max Jacques (6)	101
Kara Rabbitt (7)	102

Taelur Brentnall (6)	103
Lydia Lightfoot (6)	104
Jocelyn Trow (6)	105
Tye Holmes (7)	106
Zachary Tissié (6)	107
Erin Clark (6)	108
Finley Kinnear (7)	109
Taylor Paige Griffiths Whysall (7)	110
Kain Smith (7)	111
Beth (7)	112
Jude Hunter (6)	113
Sofia Jones (5)	114
Leland Shipley (7)	115
Chloe Redfern (6)	116
Thomas Jacob Shaw (6)	117
Alice Ellie-Mai Wheatley (6)	118
Liley Francis Hill (6)	119
Evie Hodgetts (6)	120
Owen Harris (6)	121
Bella Meeks (5)	122
Isabelle Glover (6)	123
Harry Jones (6)	124
Charlotte Richards (6)	125

St George's Primary School, Swadlincote

Layla-Jean Perry (6)	126
Olivia Grace McDermott (6)	127
Corey Harrison-Ross (6)	128
Cameron Thompson (6)	129
Max Evans (6)	130
Wiktoria Laskauska (6)	131
Oliver Clarke (6)	132
Oliver Whiten (6)	133
Amelia-Rose Bevington (6)	134
Madison Rylee Mae (6)	135
Daisy Wilson (6)	136
Maria Louise McGinty (6)	137
Henry Howlett (6)	138
Zoe Topliss (6)	139
Thomas Hadley (6)	140
Neve Edwards (6)	141
Emilia-Rose Ward (6)	142
Ronon Connor Smith (7)	143

Ashton Dooner (6) 144
Jamie Scott (6) 145

St John's CE Primary School, Ripley

Ethan Allsobrook (7) 146
Riniya Lawrence (7) 147
Noemi Skocna (7) 148
Aaron Newham (7) 149
Josh Andrews (7) 150
William Moulding (7) 151
Grace Dobson (7) 152
Alexa Jane Beighton (7) 153
Leah May Leivers (7) 154
Mitchell Gillott (6) 155
Olivia Shaw (6) 156
Sam Priest (7) 157
Marrie Chloe Medina (7) 158
Imogen Smith (7) 159
Anthony Edward Sedgwick (7) 160
Olivia Ellen Steele (7) 161
Asante Lewis Dzvene (7) 162
Libby Swanwick (7) 163
Dexter Wells (7) 164
Chloe Lea Cole (7) 165
Leah Parkin (7) 166
Riley Williams (7) 167
Sophie-Paige Walshaw 168
Porshia Boot (7) 169

St Mary's RC Primary School, Glossop

Isabel Sophie Dickson (6) 170
Melissa Crutchley (6) 171
Molly Jessica Buller (6) 172
Scarlet Findlay (6) 173
Alexi Bray (6) 174
Ethan Liang (7) 175
Layla Flanagan (6) 176
Elliott Hanks (5) 177

The Bramble Academy, Mansfield

Kacie Barker (6) 178
Lacey Louise Churchill (7) 179
Jorja Argyle (6) 180
Logan Bridgford (6) 181
Karta Riley Walker-Morgan (7) 182
Tye Boulton (6) 183

The Stories

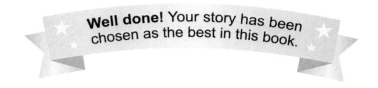

Ellie's Adventure

Ellie and Spencer arrived outside Santa's gates!
Spencer called out to another elf, 'Get the sleigh
and reindeer ready.'
A second later a big, gold sleigh with four beautiful
reindeer pulling it appeared.
Ellie got in and marvelled at the soft pink cushions.
Away they went, a bit too fast for Ellie's liking.
Soon they arrived at a big front door. Spencer got
out and knocked on the elf door knocker. The door
opened automatically. Ellie stared, open-mouthed.
Spencer said, 'Come on, Santa isn't that
important.'
'OK,' said Ellie sighing. She knew she wanted to see
Santa but she just felt frightened. Once inside all
the fright went.
They made a long journey up the stairs. Finally
Spencer and Ellie went into the room, Ellie a little
way behind.
'Oh, so you are Ellie. Spencer's told me a lot about
you.'

'How did you and Spencer know my name in the first place?' asked Ellie amazed.

'Oh I know everyone's name on the planet,' replied Santa laughing. 'Now do you want some toys?'

'Yes please,' replied Ellie.

Santa led them down a spiral staircase. Suddenly he stopped outside the door and opened it.

The room was full of toys. 'Help yourself,' said Santa.

'Really?' said Ellie.

'Really,' said Santa.

'Thank you,' said Ellie and with that she went into the room. She started taking all the toys she wanted.

Then Spencer and Ellie said goodbye to Santa and went home.

In the morning Ellie remembered her adventure. It seemed like a dream now. Then she remembered the toys. If they were somewhere, then that would mean that it had been real. She looked on the floor and saw the toys. *This means the adventure was real*, thought Ellie.

Then she heard Mum calling. 'Ellie wake up and get ready for school!'

Caitlin McCarthy

English Martyrs Catholic Primary School, Nottingham

Joe's Magical Story

At a magical place called Unicorn Land there was a giant river with silver water. In the river lived green turtles with hard brown shells and orange starfish.

Suddenly Ellie, Spencer and Herb the bear saw a giant blue dragon roaring and shooting fire at them. There was a lot of smoke.

...They felt scared so they ran away. The smoke hid them so they could escape. They ran for fifty minutes. They were exhausted.

Finally Ellie and Spencer found a unicorn called Rainbow. They rode and rode until they were in Lollipop World. They were looking for someone to help them get home.

They found a witch called Speeda who asked, 'Is everything OK?'

Ellie said, 'Can you help us get home?'

'Yes I can. Just call the broomstick.'

'Evio! Evio!'

The broomstick came - *whoosh!* They were gone in a flash and soon they were home. They were happy they were home and loved their adventure.

Joe Howie Shepherd (7)
Arnold View Primary School, Nottingham

Oscar's Magical Story

When they carefully climbed off, they found themselves in a glistening, deep ocean. They happily swam through the ocean until they came across a dark, damp cave. They worriedly got closer and closer and closer until...

They were in!

'How scary it is,' said Ellie.

'Shh, be quiet!' said Spencer.

When they were in the middle of the cave they saw two big gloomy eyes. It was a giant orange, spotty octopus!

'Who are you two?' he asked warily.

The two children were terrified of him, so much that they just couldn't speak. It was silent for a bit but then the octopus took out one of his tentacles. They were stuck! 'I'll have these two for lunch!' he said. Because of what he'd just said, he got a sharp knife.

Spencer whispered to Ellie, 'Let's get out of here.' Then when the octopus couldn't see they snuck out.

'Can you fly me home?' Ellie asked Spencer.

Spencer tried but his wings were worn out.

'What can we do now?' asked Ellie.

Spencer said, 'Nothing.' So sadly they swam back through the ocean.

Soon they saw a powerful broomstick. 'Why don't we ride on that,' said Spencer.

'Yes!' Ellie quickly replied.

When the sun started to come up they flew above the rooftops back home. What an adventure.

Oscar Straw (7)

Arnold View Primary School, Nottingham

Angel's Magical Story

Ellie was extremely excited by what she had seen. It was a unicorn the colours of the rainbow.

There was a big problem with the unicorns because they were fussing all the time. They were fussing about who had the best colour.

They were saying, 'I have the best colour because I am the queen unicorn!'

'No you don't!'

'Yes I do!'

'Stop making a fuss or someone will get you like a dragon that is red. The dragon will have hot flaming sparks coming out of his mouth.'

Then the dragon came and he had spikes and they were pink and he had stars on him. The dragon chased after them including the unicorn.

They all ran to hide behind the bushes and trees. Then Ellie and Spencer went on a broom home.

Angel Siegertsz (7)
Arnold View Primary School, Nottingham

Sadie's Magical Story

They arrived in a magical kingdom, Ellie was amazed, all of the magical creatures that she had ever read about were right here. She bent down to get closer to a ring of dancing fairies.

Suddenly a roaring red dragon appeared in front of her and Spencer! It had red fire coming out of its dangerous mouth. The red roaring dragon came chasing after Ellie and Spencer. They ran away.

The magic powers of the kingdom had brought Ellie's teddy to life, but his little legs could not run fast enough to escape the angry dragon. They jumped onto their unicorn and escaped.

'Phew!' said Ellie. 'That was close.'

The unicorn landed them in Candyland. 'Wow! Lollies. One is growing out of the ground,' said Ellie.

'No, don't touch them they belong to the warty witch!'

But it was too late, Ted was already munching on a magic lolly.

'Oi you! Hands off my garden!' screamed the nasty witch.

Sadie Gillingham (6)
Arnold View Primary School, Nottingham

Cameron's Magical Story

They arrived in a nice forest. They got off the unicorn and said thank you. They heard a loud roar, they didn't know what it was.

They looked behind them. Guess what they saw? A dragon. They shouted and ran as fast as they could and the dragon chased them.

They finally lost the dragon; they lost the dragon by throwing bread at it.

Then the unicorn came back to take them home but he ended up taking them to a witch's house and when they got there they saw a witch.

The witch chose a lollipop for them. 'Try it!' said the witch in an unkind way. All of the lollipops gave you power.

The witch forgot which lollipop gave you which power. She picked the lollipop that gave you cleverness and from the children's power they tricked the witch into eating the lollipop of kindness.

She let them go home on her broomstick.

Cameron McKay (6)
Arnold View Primary School, Nottingham

Oscar's Magical Story

Spencer and Ellie were suddenly riding on a magical unicorn with a twirling horn and a huge tail. They were riding in this land with lots of trees. Suddenly a fierce-looking dragon came out of nowhere. It scared the unicorn away.

The dragon chased the children, breathing fire. It was coming closer and closer.

Suddenly, the unicorn was back. She was charging with her head down. The dragon ran away back to its dark cave.

Soon the relieved children were back on the unicorn, riding through a colourful lollipop forest! A witch came out of nowhere and said, 'You two have had quite a scary adventure. Do you want to take one of my broomsticks to get home quickly?' 'Yes please,' said the children and they flew home.

Oscar Stanley Ryder (7)
Arnold View Primary School, Nottingham

Aimée's Magical Story

One day Ellie asked her friend Spencer the elf if they could go on an adventure on the magic carpet. Spencer said, 'Yes'. Soon they arrived at a world with unicorns and scary dragons. When they were near the unicorn part a unicorn came saying, 'Neigh,' and wanted Ellie and Spencer to climb onto its back and hold tight.

The unicorn took them to a place where they would be safe but the unicorn couldn't beat the dragon. So Ellie and Spencer tried but they were too frightened. The dragon blew some fire. So Ellie and Spencer ran as fast as they could and the dragon chased them. Then the unicorn came to save Ellie and Spencer from the evil, horrible dragon with her magic.

The magical unicorn took them to Lollipop Land to be safe. 'If you need me then scream and I'll come and save you,' said the unicorn.

'Thank you Unicorn,' said Ellie and Spencer at the same time.

When the unicorn had gone an evil witch wanted to destroy the elf and turn the girl into dinner. Then they screamed together and in a flash the unicorn came.

The unicorn then beat the witch, so Ellie and Spencer went back home to her mummy because she missed her mummy so much. She said goodbye and fell asleep straight away because she was so tired.

Aimée Marie Cooke (6)
Arnold View Primary School, Nottingham

Ruby's Magical Story

They arrived in a magical place full of the colours of the rainbow and the air around them smelled like sweets, Spiral the unicorn had magical powers.

Then they came across a dragon that breathed fire so blue that it turned everything blue, even people. Ellie and Spencer both looked like they had been dipped in blue paint.

Then Ellie, Teddy and Spencer all ran away as fast as they could because the dragon tried to eat them. So they held onto Teddy and scurried away. Just then Spiral appeared. They all got on and Spiral trotted away. They found themselves in an unusual place.

Then they saw a witch called Glinder and she let them have some of her candy and they had three candy canes that were delicious.

Glinder let them have her broomstick because they couldn't find any other way home. They landed with Teddy hanging on.

Ruby Bennett (6)
Arnold View Primary School, Nottingham

Logan's Magical Story

So they had arrived at a magical kingdom. They had got there on their magical friend Orchid Dapple, a beautiful unicorn.

Ellie and Spencer were in for a shock when they were greeted by Draco, the fire-breathing dragon. They were so scared of Draco that they ran as fast as they could away from him. Even Tilly the teddy was running.

They were so glad when they found Orchid Dapple again. They climbed on her back and continued on their journey.

Ellie, Spencer and Tilly then bumped into Trixie the witch. She was such a lovely witch they had cakes and trifles together.

Finally it was time to leave but Orchid Dapple was not around. How would they get home? Then Trixie had an idea. Ellie, Spencer and Tilly went home on Trixie's broom.

Logan Steve Evans (6)
Arnold View Primary School, Nottingham

Freya's Magical Story

Bobby and Poppy were in a forest. They met a white, pink and black unicorn. They had a ride on the unicorn. It was very fast.

Every time they saw something the unicorn disappeared. First they spotted a dragon, it looked very fierce.

They ran away from the fierce dragon. He was breathing out fire. 'Run, run for your life,' said the elf. He called the dragon, Hero.

The unicorn came back. They went over ice and jumped over lakes. They walked over paths.

They met a witch. She was very mean. The witch had a black cloak and a black hat. She had bony fingers with sharp nails.

They couldn't find the unicorn but they did find a broomstick. They flew in the window and went to bed and fell fast asleep.

Freya McNichol (6)

Arnold View Primary School, Nottingham

Darcey's Magical Story

They landed in a magical forest and rode a glamorous, colourful unicorn. The unicorn showed them around the magnificent forest.

Suddenly they saw a big, red dragon. So they ran deep into the magical forest. Little did they know the dragon was following them.

They ran and ran until they lost the dragon. 'Phew!' said Ellie. 'That was a close one!'

The sun was beating down as they rode happily along the big, green forest.

They saw a dark side of the forest so they went in it and there was a black gate. They went in the gate and there was a witch.

The witch saw Ellie and Spencer were tired so she let them ride on her fast brown broomstick all the way home.

Darcey Walker (6)
Arnold View Primary School, Nottingham

Freya's Magical Story

They arrived in a land called Zootrakalist, a land with unicorns. Ellie held tight to Spencer as they flew over cities.

Afterwards they went to a dragon world. 'Ellie!' cried Spencer. 'Look out!'

There was a very scary, hungry dragon.

They ran away from the scary dragon. 'Oh help!' said Spencer the elf. But then Rosetta the unicorn came and rescued Ellie and Spencer. The dragon ran away but Rosetta froze him with her icy magic. After that they were very hungry and they came to a sweetie house and they started to eat it and a witch came out with her broom and chased them. Ellie took the broom out of the witch's hand and they flew back home.

Freya Wilson (6)
Arnold View Primary School, Nottingham

Ameliya's Magical Story

Ellie jumped on the back of Spencer's beautiful white unicorn, heading to the dark spooky mountain.

When out of nowhere came the angriest fire-breathing dragon. Ellie and Spencer screamed very loudly.

The dragon was very angry and didn't want them in his mountains so he breathed a big breath of fire towards them.

After running away very fast they were happy to get their breath back whilst riding the unicorn.

Then a scary witch appeared and gave them sweets. She was a nice witch and had come to help them.

She lent them her broomstick so they could fly home fast and safe.

Ameliya Logan (6)

Arnold View Primary School, Nottingham

Lara's Magical Story

Ellie and Spencer went to a magical place where nobody has ever been.

When they arrived they felt scared because a green, mean and deadly dragon was standing in front of them and he was breathing really hot fire.

Ellie and Spencer and Ellie's little teddy ran as fast as they could to get away from the deadly, fire-breathing dragon.

They saw the beautiful, soft unicorn and jumped onto her to get away.

When she dropped them off they saw a wicked, ugly witch and she lived in a candyfloss and chocolate and sweetie house.

They snatched the broomstick from her and rode home.

Lara Gingell (7)
Arnold View Primary School, Nottingham

Samuel's Magical Story

At a magical pony town we asked a pony if we could ride on his back. Then we saw a portal.

We went through it and suddenly we stood in front of a fierce dragon and it made the teddy come alive.

Then the three of us ran as fast as we could and bumped into a door. We went through the door as fast as we could.

We landed back on a pony and trotted off into the forest and we found...

An evil witch. She said, 'Come with me you three!' Then she whispered, 'I'm going to eat you.'

We overheard what the witch said and so we stole her broom to ride back home.

Samuel Ridley (5)

Arnold View Primary School, Nottingham

Dominic's Magical Story

In a dark scary forest they found a path made of sugar lumps.

They saw a dragon who caused fire that was scary to be near.

Ellie, Spencer and Teddy didn't think he looked friendly and ran away.

They ran back to the unicorn who took them up a hill.

They saw lollipops and knew that there had to be a witch. She was kind and gave the teddy a lollipop.

They stayed for a cup of tea and then Teddy was tired so they used the witch's broom to go back home.

Dominic Carey (6)

Arnold View Primary School, Nottingham

Olivia's Magical Story

At the magical kingdom of elves, there were unicorns, elves and castles.
Suddenly behind them there was a dragon breathing out fire. The dragon was terrifying.
The dragon was chasing the kids and also the teddy bear. They were scared.
The unicorn ran as fast as it could and the children jumped on it as fast as they could.
Then the children met a witch and the witch tried to capture the children.
The children flew away at night on the magic broom.

Olivia Leman (6)

Arnold View Primary School, Nottingham

Grace's Magical Story

Ellie and Spencer set off on their adventure. They walked down a pink path and they found a unicorn and her name was Rainbow. She had rainbow hair. There was a big dragon and they were looking for a crystal and they got it.

Ellie and Spencer ran away and the dragon lost them.

The unicorn rode Ellie and Spencer to Candyland.

There was a witch at Candyland. Ellie and Spencer took the broom from her.

Ellie and Spencer flew back to bed.

Grace Wallis (7)

Arnold View Primary School, Nottingham

Ollie's Magical Story

They arrived at Barcelona Stadium, it was such a surprise! Ellie had never seen a stadium before. Spencer and Ellie walked onto the pitch. They were scared as a dragon appeared in front of them. They ran and ran so fast.

They got out of Barcelona Stadium and a unicorn came to rescue them.

Soon a witch jumped out of a bush.

While the witch wasn't looking Ellie and Spencer grabbed her broom and zoomed off.

Ollie Rothwell (7)

Arnold View Primary School, Nottingham

Joshua's Magical Story

Once upon a time Hansel and Gretel were in the woods. A unicorn said, 'Can I take you to Candyland?'
But they got lost and ended up at the monster's house.
The monster chased them but a magical teddy rescued them.
The unicorn flew them to Candyland.
But they weren't out of danger yet. A wicked witch tried to trick them.
But they stole her broom and flew home.

Joshua Coleman (6)
Arnold View Primary School, Nottingham

Kiaya's Magical Story

Soon they arrived at Unicorn Land. They saw an elf with white ears. The unicorn had never seen an elf before.

After that they saw a girl called Little Red Riding Hood, she had some cupcakes. They had some hundreds and thousands on them.

They went to see Grandma. It was a long adventure.

After that Little Red Riding Hood lost her teddy. She was worried. She cried for the unicorn and he felt sorry for her. When they got to Grandma's house she wasn't there. She was upset again. The unicorn said, 'I feel sorry for you again.' Then they had another walk.

The elf saw a house with a sign on saying: 'Oak Tree'. 'That's Grandma's house,' said Ellie.

Kiaya Bartlett (7)
Arnold View Primary School, Nottingham

Ellie And Spencer's Adventure

Ellie and Spencer arrived in the telly room. 'Why are we in here?' asked Ellie.

Spencer got out the dobber and pressed a button - *zoom!* They zoomed inside the TV and arrived in a blocky land that had trees, caves and a village.

'Come over here!' said Spencer. 'There's somebody called Timmy here. He lives in this village and he is a very friendly villager. Hello Timmy,' said Spencer, 'how are you?'

'I'm fine,' said Timmy. He was cooking some pork chops on his furnace. 'Except for the creepers apocalypse.'

'What are creepers?' asked Ellie.

'Creepers,' said Timmy, 'are creatures that blow everything up. They come every Friday and, oh no it's Friday today! You need to get prepared.'

'How do we get prepared?' asked Ellie and Spencer.

'There's a cave around here that has lots of diamonds in it.'

'OK, let's go to the cave!'

Soon they arrived at the cave. They went down and immediately spotted diamonds. They instantly started mining them and soon made diamond armour and all sorts. It was about this time that the creepers came charging down the hill. Spencer and Ellie saw them and killed them all. There were some signs that said: 'You need to kill the half-wither, half-ender dragon!'

Spencer and Ellie saw a portal and they jumped in it and there was the almighty dragon. They charged in and killed it. They jumped back through the portal but Ellie didn't know how to get home. 'I know,' said Spencer, 'I can build a dragon and you can fly home.' Spencer finally built it and Ellie flew home gracefully.

'Bye Spencer, see you soon!'

Findlay Parker (7)

English Martyrs Catholic Primary School, Nottingham

Ellie And Spencer's Beach Adventure

Ellie and Spencer arrived at the beautiful and sunny beach.

'What's that over there?' asked Ellie.

'Oh, that's just my pet dolphin swimming in the blue smooth sea. Would you like to meet him?'

'Yes please,' said Ellie.

The pet swam over to Ellie and spoke to her. 'Get on my back and I will give you a ride,' said the pet.

'OK,' said Ellie.

Ellie and Spencer climbed onto the dolphin's back and had a ride. While the dolphin was giving them a ride they saw a mermaid and went over to her. The mermaid asked, 'Would you like to come under the sea and have a party?'

'Yes please,' Spencer the elf and Ellie said.

At the party they had seafood and even had a disco. They met lots of sea creatures including a jellyfish and a stingray. It grew dark so they swam back to shore. Spencer felt different. Ellie looked at him and he was a human.

'I've always wanted to be a human,' he said. 'I'm giving you some magic dust to fly home.'
'Thank you,' said Ellie. She flew back home, got into bed and was getting ready for another lovely day with Spencer.

Roisin Parker (7)

English Martyrs Catholic Primary School, Nottingham

Abigail's Space Story

They went to space and she brought her teddy too.
They flew out of the Earth. 'It's amazing,' said Ellie.
They landed on the moon with a thump.
They met an alien called Bob. Bob said, 'Collect stars to bring home.'
So they did. They played with Bob and they played hide-and-seek.
Bob said to Ellie and Spencer the elf, 'Come in my flying saucer.'
'Have you got Teddy?' said Ellie.
'Don't worry,' said Bob, 'I've got him here!'
They flew away in the flying saucer. 'Hello,' said Ellie to some other aliens. 'Look at all the stars. Down a little more!' So they went down.
'Oh no Sticky Tongue,' Bob said. Sticky Tongue has a very sticky and long tongue. 'Oh no, we're stuck! Pull and pull and pull, yay!'
'Bye-bye,' said Bob and Ellie and Spencer.
So Ellie walked and walked till she got to the house and she said, 'Night, night everyone.'

Abigail Newman (6)
English Martyrs Catholic Primary School, Nottingham

Isaac's Space Story

They arrived in space. Spencer said, 'Shall we go on a planet?'

'Yes,' said Ellie.

'But which one?' said Spencer.

'The moon please.'

They started collecting stars on the way.

An alien was watching them. Ellie saw him and she said, 'What's your name Mister Alien?'

'My name is Joel,' Joel said, 'do you want a ride in my spaceship?'

Suddenly a monster captured them but they got free.

Then the spaceship dropped her off. 'Goodbye!' said Ellie.

Isaac Jules Brown (6)
English Martyrs Catholic Primary School, Nottingham

Isabella's Jungle Story

Ellie and Spencer arrived at the jungle. They were walking but then they came across a big river and they couldn't find a way to get across. But then they saw some long, wavy green vines. 'Let's swing across!' said Ellie.

'What a great idea that is.'

So they swung across safely and happily. When they got to the other side, they heard a scary hissing sound. 'What could that be?' said Spencer. Then they looked in the green bush and there was a scary snake. It was looking at them very curiously

Ellie and Spencer were very scared. 'What shall we do?' Then the snake hissed in anger. 'Run!' they said. 'Run away from the snake!'

Finally they got away and next they met a friendly tiger. 'Would you like to go for a ride?'

'Yes please!'

The tiger's name was Henry. He was big, yellow and brave. The tiger was very friendly. Ellie and Spencer were very excited to ride a tiger. They travelled back through the jungle. They saw lots of interesting animals. Small, big, tall and short animals. They even saw another tiger. They said, 'Thank you for the ride!'

They then swung across the green wavy vines.
They were flying across the streets once again.
What a lovely flight home.
'Bye,' said Ellie, 'see you for another adventure.'

Isabella Syson (7)

English Martyrs Catholic Primary School, Nottingham

The Magic Volcano

Ellie and Spencer arrived at the rim of an erupting, magic volcano! First of all they had to dodge hot bubbling magma and lava. Then they met Tom, Elena and Ferno. Ferno soon saw Epos and Togus. Togus had special hooves put on to help him withstand the hot lava. Ellie, Spencer and Tom rode the three good beasts all over England. What a great sight it was. Ellie rode on Ferno and Spencer caught four of Epos' feathers to help them deal with the heat. Tom was following them just in case anything happened to them, nothing did happen to them until the very top! It was full of blue, green and red lava. Ellie thought it was beautiful. Soon a multicoloured stone warrior rose from the deep but it slowly turned to black then to grey and was evil!

Tom asked, 'Do you want my shield?'

'Yes,' answered Spencer before loads more weaker terracotta warriors rose, all carrying weapons.

Ellie reached out to each one but Elena called out, 'Don't touch them!'

Then Spencer handed the shield to Ellie and a terracotta attacked but missed. Phew! Suddenly Epos the flame bird dropped a fireball on the chief before he disappeared and reappeared behind Ellie.

As Spencer touched one his body became encased in stone! Tom struck the great stone army and huge terrifying leader with his sharp steel sword so they turned back to their normal selves.
Ellie and Spencer rode Togus back home. Ellie and Spencer were happy to be home.

Charlie Gooch (7)
English Martyrs Catholic Primary School, Nottingham

Ellie And Spencer's Wonderful Adventure

Ellie and Spencer arrived at a beautiful, magical land. Then, Ellie and Spencer jumped on a rainbow-coloured unicorn! Suddenly a huge fierce dragon ran up to both of them and breathed fire at them! After that Ellie and Spencer got extremely scared, they ran away.

Then they got on another unicorn and galloped away really, really quickly.

Next, they saw a house made of all the sweeties you could think of. At that moment a wicked witch came out of it and said, 'Come in, I will look after you.'

'No,' said Ellie quietly.

'Come on, I will give you a sweetie,' she said.

Then Spencer had an idea. When she wasn't looking they would get on her broomstick and fly home. When Ellie got home she snuggled down into bed and fell fast asleep.

Sophie Ellen Collins (7)

English Martyrs Catholic Primary School, Nottingham

Obinna's Magical Story

Wow! They went on a unicorn. They flew off, it took some time to get there and a few hours too.

When they got there they saw a dragon. It was blowing out fire. Ellie and Spencer were very scared. The dragon had very, very sharp claws and pointy teeth.

Ellie and Spencer the elf ran away from the dragon and so did Ellie's teddy. Ellie said to Spencer, 'That dragon was terrifying!'

So they got back on the unicorn and travelled back. Spencer said, 'We are having a nice time!'

Then a wicked witch came up and pointed to Ellie and Spencer and the wicked witch laughed at Ellie and Spencer.

Then Ellie and Spencer the elf went back to their houses and went back to bed.

Obinna Dale Okwuolisa (6)

English Martyrs Catholic Primary School, Nottingham

Imogen's Magical Story

They met a cute, fluffy unicorn. He let them have a ride. He had a beautiful pink horn. He had lovely coal black hooves and yellow skin.

They saw a big, scary dragon. They got very, very scared. Ellie's teddy hid behind Ellie's back and was also very, very scared.

They ran away as fast as their little legs could go. They got very, very scared.

They saw the unicorn again and they were very happy. He had a very, very bright red tail.

Who do you think Ellie and Spencer will meet next? They met a wicked witch and she scared them.

They took her broom and got on the broom they stole. Spencer took Ellie home on the broomstick.

Imogen Rose Burn (6)

English Martyrs Catholic Primary School, Nottingham

Bethany's Jungle Story

As if by magic they were swinging through the trees on vines. Even Ellie's teddy went on the adventure.

Suddenly the vines snapped and they found out they were standing in front of a big, scary snake and they felt very scared.

How did they get away from the snake? They got away by running. What did they see next?

Next they saw a big, friendly lion and they were all shocked. Even his mane looked friendly.

The lion let them all have a ride through the jungle and he stopped when they got to some vines.

They swung on the vines home but where was Ellie's teddy...? Then Spencer saw him. He was on Ellie's back!

Bethany Dooley-Roberts (6)

English Martyrs Catholic Primary School, Nottingham

William's Zoo Story

One night Ellie was woken by a tap on the window! It was Spencer the elf and he said, 'Do you want to go on an adventure?'

When they got to the zoo they met an elephant. The big elephant gave them a ride. Then they met a crunchy panda.

The panda was very fluffy and cuddly. Ellie cuddled the panda and it cuddled her.

They jumped on the elephant again and on the way they saw some hairy monkeys and they were very, very, very cheeky.

Ellie saw a gorilla and he was eating a banana. Ellie liked bananas so she ate one too!

Ellie had to say goodbye to Spencer the elf. She was so tired and had to get back to her bed.

William Crannage (6)
English Martyrs Catholic Primary School, Nottingham

Phoebe's Magical Story

They went to a magical land. Then they saw a unicorn! Spencer and Ellie had a ride on the unicorn.

When they got off the unicorn they saw a dragon and Ellie's teddy hid behind Ellie's back.

They all ran away from the dragon because he was breathing fire. The dragon was mean as well.

Then they got back on the unicorn and they rode away on the road on the unicorn in the hot sun.

When they got off the unicorn again they saw a witch and the witch was mean and nasty.

Ellie said, 'It is time for me to go home and get some sleep but tomorrow we can have another adventure!'

Phoebe Hamilton (6)

English Martyrs Catholic Primary School, Nottingham

Luca's Pirate Story

They were in an old wooden boat. Spencer saw a big, enormous boat with people on it. They came closer and closer and they were pirates.

They were good pirates though.

One pirate gave them some money. 'Thank you,' they said.

Then he made them walk the plank, Spencer was first. Ellie wanted to help him but she knew it would be no use so they both walked the plank. Then they got on a dolphin which took them to the shore. They both said thank you to the dolphin. They began to walk back together and when they got home they said goodbye.

Luca Abraham (6)
English Martyrs Catholic Primary School, Nottingham

Molly's Jungle Story

Ellie and Spencer arrived in the jungle.
Spencer showed Ellie how to swing on thick vines.
Then they saw a fast flowing river up ahead.
Spencer told Ellie that she needed to use the vines to swing across the river. Ellie was scared because she thought she might fall in. She didn't fall in, she got to the other side safely.
When they had walked a little further into the jungle they saw a snake and it was tangled up. Ellie didn't know if she should help the snake. Suddenly the snake started to move.
'Run!' shouted Spencer. 'It's going to eat us.'
Then Ellie saw a lion and asked if she could have a ride and he said yes. Then Ellie and Spencer climbed onto some vines and headed back home. Ellie climbed into bed and snuggled with her teddy and soon she was fast asleep.

Molly Campbell (7)

English Martyrs Catholic Primary School, Nottingham

Hugo's Pirate Story

Spencer took Ellie on a boat to an island and on that island there was a box and what was in it? There was a box of treasure with pure gold inside it and other gold things were inside it. Then there was a pirate ship and the man came off the pirate ship and shouted, 'Argh! Who dares to enter my case of gold?'

The pirate took Ellie and the elf on the pirate ship and made Spencer walk the plank. Ellie was scared for Spencer walking the plank.

Then Ellie and Spencer jumped onto a dolphin and then Spencer took Ellie home.

Hugo Daft (6)

English Martyrs Catholic Primary School, Nottingham

Ellie And Spencer's Jungle Adventure

Ellie and Spencer arrived at the jungle.

First they swung on the ropes with Ellie's teddy bear. Next when they walked further they saw a big, long, snake, he smiled and he was tied up so Ellie helped the snake by untying his tail and they ran away.

After this they saw a lion. They rode on it. It was very fast and they decided to go home so they went back on the ropes together.

Soon they were back home. Spencer the elf went back home too. Ellie's teddy bear enjoyed the adventure.

Victoria Kozak (7)

English Martyrs Catholic Primary School, Nottingham

Charlie's Magical Story

They saw a unicorn arrive, it was cute. 'I like it. I love you,' said Ellie.

They saw a dragon, they thought it was nasty as it was breathing fire.

They were scared so they ran away. It nearly got them. 'Come on! Are you coming?' said the elf.

They rode away on the unicorn.

'Mummy, I love you. What is that behind your back?'

Mummy turned into a witch who said, 'I'm going to eat you.'

They flew to their grandma's house.

Charlie Sarah Webster (6)
Heath Primary School, Chesterfield

Charlie's Magical Story

In Magical World they saw a pony in front of them.
They hopped on and went up a mountain. They
were scared so they ran away.
They saw a dragon and it was bad. The blue ninja
came and got out his weapon.
They ran away from the dragon.
They went back on the pony.
They saw a witch, she said, 'He, he, he! Do you
need my broom?'
'Yes,' they said.
Then they went home.

Charlie Wills (5)
Heath Primary School, Chesterfield

Seth's Magical Story

Ellie and Spencer saw a unicorn called Milly. Milly was so fluffy. The unicorn was so fluffy. Ellie and Spencer wanted to stay.

Next they found a fire-breathing dragon and Ellie was scared. They were so scared they fell over. They had to run away from the fire-breathing dragon. The dragon was catching up with them. The magical unicorn took them somewhere exciting. Ellie and Spencer were excited to get home.

Next they saw a wicked witch who gave them a broomstick. They found out that the witch was nice.

Ellie and Spencer flew back home. Ellie went back to bed. Ellie said goodbye to Spencer.

Seth Melluish (6)
Heath Primary School, Chesterfield

Gracie's Magical Story

Ellie and Spencer were on a unicorn. The unicorn was a baby unicorn called Rose.

Ellie and Spencer saw a fire-breathing dragon. But luckily the baby unicorn Rose saw them getting attacked so she saved them.

Ellie and Spencer were so scared. They ran away from the fire-breathing dragon.

Ellie and Spencer got back on the unicorn and the unicorn took Ellie and Spencer to a kind little witch. When Ellie and Spencer saw the witch they were not very sure whether the witch was good or bad. The witch let Ellie and Spencer take a broom to have a ride home.

Gracie Lei Fox (6)
Heath Primary School, Chesterfield

Olivia's Magical Story

Ellie and Spencer had a ride on a unicorn and her name was Daisy. She had a really sparkly horn with lots of magic.

Then a fire-breathing dragon came and scared them with its hot boiling fire.

Ellie and Spencer ran as fast as they could but the dragon was catching them up.

Next the unicorn was taking them to a nice kind witch. Soon they were there.

Then the nice witch gave them her broomstick.

Next they flew home with a whoosh and went back to bed.

Olivia Denham (6)
Heath Primary School, Chesterfield

Ashton's Space Story

Spencer asked Ellie if she wanted to go to outer space but they hadn't seen the alien.

Then they landed on the moon and had a game of catch the stars.

Suddenly the alien caught them and they went in the spaceship.

Then the alien was kind to them in the spaceship.

Then something was under the spaceship. It was a monster. It had a long tongue.

Ellie went back to her house and she went back to bed.

Ashton Kieran James Pollard (6)

Heath Primary School, Chesterfield

Liam's Zoo Story

Spencer woke Ellie up then Spencer took Ellie to the zoo. They went in the zoo.

They went on an elephant and they rode the elephant all about.

Spencer cuddled a baby panda. Ellie cuddled an adult panda and Tatty Teddy.

The elephant took Ellie and Spencer to see more animals.

Ellie ate a banana with a monkey. Tatty Teddy was climbing.

Then Spencer rode the elephant home.

Liam Milner (6)

Heath Primary School, Chesterfield

Isabella's Magical Story

At Fairy Land they feel happy, at Fairy Land they meet a unicorn.

Then a dragon came and scared them - the dragon was breathing fire.

They ran away because the dragon was breathing lots of fire.

They went to find the unicorn and got back on the unicorn.

After this they met a witch, she had pointy nails.

They snatched the broomstick and flew home.

Isabella O'Brien-Smith (6)
Heath Primary School, Chesterfield

Maisie's Magical Story

Ellie and Spencer went on a unicorn.

Ellie and Spencer got off the unicorn and they saw a dragon. Then they got on the unicorn again. Then they ran away from the dragon.

Then they got on the unicorn again.

They saw a good witch. 'You can get on the broomstick,' she said.

Then they got home with the broomstick with Teddy, Ellie and Spencer.

Maisie Jean (5)
Heath Primary School, Chesterfield

Jasmine's Magical Story

In Pony Land the children rode on the pony.
A dragon was breathing fire and the children were scared.
The children ran away from the dragon.
The pony gave them a ride back home. The children and the horse went flying off.
Teddy was licking a lolly. The candy had turned Teddy to chocolate.
The children went on the broomstick and went home to bed.

Jasmine Power (6)
Heath Primary School, Chesterfield

Harvey's Jungle Story

One night Ellie and Spencer were in the jungle. They were swinging on vines.

Ellie and Spencer met a snake. The snake said, 'I want to eat you.'

Ellie and Spencer ran away from the snake.

Ellie met a lion. The lion was big and his name was Lion Ryan.

The lion let them have a ride on his back.

Spencer took Ellie home. Ellie said goodbye.

Harvey David Fox (6)
Heath Primary School, Chesterfield

David's Space Story

They went into space with Ellie's teddy. They could see Earth.

They went to collect stars on an alien ship. He saw them.

They went into a ship. It was the alien ship.

They went exploring in space, they were still in the ship.

The monster was going to eat them but he floated away.

They then dropped Ellie at home.

David Peter Munks (5)
Heath Primary School, Chesterfield

Jodie's Magical Story

Ellie and Spencer got on the unicorn.

Ellie and Spencer were frightened of the dragon. A really big dragon.

They ran away from the dragon

Spencer and Ellie got on the unicorn and flew away.

They met a friendly witch who saved them and gave them a broomstick to ride home.

They went back home for their dinner.

Jodie Marie Dale (6)
Heath Primary School, Chesterfield

Melisa's Magical Story

Ellie and Spencer were on a unicorn.
The dragon breathed fire at Ellie and Spencer.
They ran away from the dragon. They were scared.
Then the unicorn saved them from the dragon.
Then they saw a nice witch. The witch told the broom to take them home.
Ellie and Spencer went home. They felt happy.

Melisa Atmaca (6)
Heath Primary School, Chesterfield

Lorna's Magical Story

In Magic Land they were happy.

They saw a dragon and they were scared.

They ran away from the dragon.

They got back on their unicorn.

Then they saw a witch and they thought she was a nasty witch.

But she wasn't. Then they went on the witch's broomstick back to Magic Land.

Lorna Dawn Walmsley (6)

Heath Primary School, Chesterfield

Archie's Jungle Story

They arrived in the jungle and when they got there they swung on the vines.

They had a swing about and then they saw a snake.

They ran away and hid in a bush.

When they got in the bush they saw a tiger.

They rode on the tiger.

Then they got off the tiger and they had to go home.

Archie Potter (6)

Heath Primary School, Chesterfield

Marcus' Magical Story

Ellie and Spencer were on the unicorn, they took off to an island.
The dragon burned fire.
They ran away from the dragon.
The unicorn was called William.
There was a witch who was a nice witch. The witch let them have her broom.
They had tea when they flew home.

Marcus Banerjee (5)
Heath Primary School, Chesterfield

Ellie's Magical Story

Ellie and Spencer rode on a unicorn.

Ellie and Spencer saw a dragon.

They ran away from the dragon.

The got on the unicorn.

They met a witch and she was a good witch.

The witch let them go on her broom so they flew home.

Ellie Grace (6)

Heath Primary School, Chesterfield

Zack's Magical Story

One day a unicorn came to their house.
Then they saw a dragon and they were scared.
They ran away and the dragon was catching up.
But the unicorn came.
They went to the witch's house.
Then they went home on a broom.

Zack Banner (6)
Heath Primary School, Chesterfield

Riley's Jungle Story

They went to the jungle, they swung on the vines.
They saw a really big snake.
The snake stopped. The snake was kind again.
The tiger was kind, they went on his back.
They thought it was fun.
Then they went home.

Riley Cowie (6)
Heath Primary School, Chesterfield

Isla's Space Story

They went up above into space. They wanted to catch some stars then an alien snuck up on them. They did not see the alien, they were just catching stars and did not notice. The alien got in his space flying saucer.

Ellie got caught into the flying saucer and Spencer did as well but they had so much fun flying around in the spacecraft and even Tatty Teddy loved it.

Then they saw a three-eyed alien and it had a long tongue and pointy teeth. They were scared of the alien. But Tatty Teddy enjoyed it and he was not frightened.

Then Ellie and Spencer and the alien all went home.

Isla Amans (6)
Heath Primary School, Chesterfield

Ruby's Story

They arrived at the beach. It is fun making sandcastles and swimming in the deep, deep water and scary dark water.

'Hello Ellie,' said the crab, 'do you want to go to my party? Only joking. I'm going to eat you!'

'Now! Now! Let's run away from the crab.'

'Hello Ice Cream Man, can I have an ice cream please because I'm so hungry and starving.'

'Fine, you can have an ice cream.'

'Hi Ellie, what are you eating?' said Spencer.

'An ice cream!' said Ellie.

'Oh,' said Spencer, 'can I have an ice cream please?'

'Yes.'

'This is fun,' said Spencer and Ellie.

'What are you doing, Spencer?'

'Making a sandcastle like you told me to and it's fun.'

'It's time to go home and I'm supposed to go home,' said Spencer. 'Bye Ellie!'

Ruby Richardson (6)

Mellers Primary School, Nottingham

Spencer And Ellie Have Fun At The Beach

Spencer and Ellie arrived at the sunny beach and it was wonderful. Spencer found a tennis ball. They played catch with it and then Ellie had a swim in the blue ocean. Ellie found some beautiful fish in the ocean and swam with them.

Suddenly Ellie saw a gargantuan grey shark! He had very sharp teeth. 'I'm going to eat you!' said the shark.

'Argh!' Ellie swam as fast as she could back to the beach.

'Are you alright?' asked Spencer.

'Yes, but I just got chased by a massive shark!' gasped Ellie.

'Oh!' said Spencer.

They played football and Ellie won 2-1. They had a walk around the beach.

'This is a fantastic day!' said Ellie. 'Can I do some more fun things with you?'

'Yes,' said Spencer.

Ellie and Spencer went surfing in the ocean and Spencer was the best. A big huge wave came and Spencer surfed right to the top of it.

They went back onto the hot beach and sunbathed on the sand with sunglasses on. The tide started to come in and it got cold.

'Time to go,' said Spencer.

Then they flew back home.

Omar Nyandou (6)

Mellers Primary School, Nottingham

Joshua's Story

Soon they had arrived at the city. 'What shall we do?' said Spencer. Then they had an idea. They did lots of stuff until they ran out of ideas.

Then suddenly they met a kind policeman and said, 'Hello, who are you?'

Spencer looked confused.

'Let's leave him alone,' said Spencer.

'Do you want to go in the police station?' said the kind policeman.

'Yes,' said Spencer, 'but remember what I said.'

'Yes, but he's so kind,' said Ellie, so Spencer said nothing.

'Just come in,' said the policeman.

'No,' said Spencer.

But before he could say it Ellie jumped right in, 'Yes,' she said. So they went in.

When they went in they were shocked. 'How long has this been up for?' said Spencer.

'Time to go home,' said Spencer. So they went home.

Joshua Rozee (6)
Mellers Primary School, Nottingham

Hamza's Jungle Story

They went in the jungle. They swung on the vines. Then they saw a snake. They snake said, 'Do you want to go to a party?'

They were not sure, but then they said, 'Yes.'

Suddenly Ellie said, 'Where is the party?'

'I was only joking. I'm going to eat you!'

The snake was chasing Ellie and Spencer. 'Run away!'

Then they heard a roaring voice. It was a friendly lion. The lion said, 'Do you want to have a ride?'

'Yes.'

'Where do you want to go?'

'Through the jungle,' they said.

Time to go home.

Hamza Mehmood (6)
Mellers Primary School, Nottingham

Nevaeh's Story

When they got there Ellie said, 'Why are we at the park?'

Spencer didn't say anything.

While they were at the park Ellie played on the slide. She said, 'Whee!'

Spencer wanted a turn.

Suddenly a mean kidnapper called Dillan appeared. Ellie and Spencer said, 'Argh!'

Dillan took them to jail.

Ellie said, 'Let us out!'

Dillan said, 'No.'

Luckily Spencer had his magic fairy wand to let them out so they got away.

Dillan shouted, 'No, they've got away!'

So they flew back home where they were safe.

Nevaeh Regan-Turner (6)

Mellers Primary School, Nottingham

Diwan's Story

Spencer and Ellie arrived at the city. First they jumped over the rooftops. Then they went in the houses and buildings. 'This is great,' said Ellie. Then they went to the hospital. Suddenly a car crashed into Spencer. 'Argh!' said Spencer.

The hospital took Spencer inside and Spencer felt better.

After they went to the scary police station. After the police station they went to the prison. A stranger came to put Spencer in the prison. Ellie got Spencer.

'Wait! Let Spencer go!' she said.

Spencer went there.

Then the stranger went to jail. 'Yay!' said Spencer and Ellie.

Spencer went to the ice cream van. Spencer wanted chocolate ice cream. Ellie wanted vanilla ice cream.

Ellie and Spencer went to the shop to get some food. Then Spencer went to the park. Ellie went on the slide and Spencer went on the swings.

'Time to go home!' said Spencer. Then they flew all the way home.

Diwan Sherif (6)

Mellers Primary School, Nottingham

Jasmine's Jungle Story

They had arrived in the deep jungle. They swung on some long thin vines. Ellie liked to swing.

Suddenly they saw a sneaky, scary snake! 'Do you want to come to my birthday party?' said the snake.

'Yes please,' said Ellie, 'but where is the birthday party?'

'Only joking. I'm going to eat you.'

'Argh!' said Ellie and Spencer.

Suddenly they heard a loud roar. It was a big friendly lion. 'Do you want to go for a ride?' said the lion.

'Yes please!'

'It's fun,' said Spencer and Ellie.

'I'm enjoying this ride,' said Spencer.

'It's time to go,' said Ellie. So they went home.

Jasmine Sobiesinska (6)

Mellers Primary School, Nottingham

Yasmin's Jungle Story

They had arrived in a deep jungle. They swung on the long thin vines. 'This is fun!' said Ellie. *Ellie loves to swing*, thought Spencer.

Suddenly they saw a sneaky, scary snake! 'Do you want to come to a birthday party?'

'OK. But where is the party?'

'Just pretending. I am going to eat you.'

'Argh! Run!' said Ellie.

But then they saw a friendly lion. 'Do you want to come for a ride?'

'Yes please,' said Ellie.

'It's so much fun. Thank you,' said Ellie.

'You're welcome!'

They swung on the long thin vines. It was time to go back home.

Yasmin Elayeb (6)
Mellers Primary School, Nottingham

Halima's Jungle Story

They arrived in the jungle. They swung through the jungle. They looked down and they saw a snake. The snake was trapped. Ellie said, 'Shall we help the snake?'

'Yes, let's be kind.'

'Oh OK.'

So they untied the snake.

'What shall we get to help the snake?' The snake knew how to get out.

The snake chased Ellie and the elf. 'Argh! Help!'

After this they saw a friendly lion. The lion said, 'Do you want a ride?'

'Yes.'

So they had a ride. 'This is such fun and it is the best day ever.'

'It's time to go home. See you next time!'

Halima Jammeh (5)

Mellers Primary School, Nottingham

Aween's Jungle Story

They went to the jungle. They swung on the long vines. 'This is fun,' said Ellie.

Next they saw a sneaky snake. 'Would you like to come to my party?'

They were not sure. 'OK.'

'Only joking. I'm going to eat you!'

They ran away from the snake!

Next they saw a lion. 'Do you want to come for a ride?'

'Yes please!'

So they went on his back. 'This is fun,' said Ellie.

'It's time to go home,' said Spencer.

So they swung through the green jungle and went home.

Aween Fatah (6)

Mellers Primary School, Nottingham

Nour's Jungle Story

They swung on the vines.

Then they met a snake.

'Would you like to come to a party?'

'Yes,' said Ellie and Spencer, 'but where is the party?'

'This is where!'

'Argh!' said Ellie and Spencer.

Then they met a lion. 'Would you like to come on a ride?' said the lion.

'Yes,' said Ellie and Spencer.

'Whee!' said Ellie and Spencer. 'This is fun.'

'It's time to go home,' said Spencer.

Nour Zurqani (5)

Mellers Primary School, Nottingham

Ahmed's Jungle Story

They swung on the vines. The vines swung. They swung on the vines so they could go to the jungle. Then they met a snake who said, 'Do you want to go to a party?'

'Where is the party?'

'I am joking. I am going to eat you.'

The snake scared them so they ran away from the snake.

Then they met a lion. He was a friendly lion. He was learning to be good.

The lion said, 'Do you want a ride?'

They said, 'Yes.'

'It's time to go home. It's time to go to bed. Goodnight!'

Ahmed Salama (6)

Mellers Primary School, Nottingham

Fahim's Jungle Story

They swung on the vines. 'This is fun,' said Ellie.
Suddenly Ellie met a sneaky snake. 'Do you want to go to a party?'
'OK,' said the snake.
'Run away,' said Spencer the elf.
'Roar!' said the friendly lion.
'Hello, who are you?' said Ellie.
'Do you want to go on a ride?' said the friendly lion.
So they ran through the jungle.
'It's time to go home,' said Ellie and Spencer the elf.

Fahim Ali (6)

Mellers Primary School, Nottingham

Mohammed's Jungle Story

They had arrived in the deep jungle. Then they swung on the long thin vines.
'Would you like to come to my party?'
The children were not scared. 'Where is the party?'
'I am going to eat you.'
They ran away from the slippery snake.
They saw a friendly lion.
'Would you like to go on a ride?'
'Yes please,' said the children.
Spencer said, 'It's time to go home.'

Mohammed Abodhir (6)
Mellers Primary School, Nottingham

Binta's Jungle Story

They arrived at the jungle and they swung on the vines with the bear.

Suddenly a sneaky snake said to Ellie, Spencer and the bear, 'Would you like to go to a party?'

'Yes,' said Ellie.

'Where is the party?' asked Ellie and Spencer.

'I'm going to eat you!'

Next they saw a friendly lion. 'Would you like to have a ride?'

Then they climbed on the friendly lion and they went on to have a fun time.

'Time to go home,' said Ellie. So they went home.

Binta Danso (6)

Mellers Primary School, Nottingham

Mohammed's Jungle Story

They arrived at the jungle. They swung on the long vines. When they got there they saw a mysterious snake. The snake slithered.

'Do you want to come to my party? ...I was only joking,' said the snake, 'there is no party.'

'Run away,' said Spencer.

They met a friendly lion. 'Do you want to go on a ride?'

'Thank you,' said Spencer and Ellie.

'This is fun,' said Spencer.

They swung on the vines all the way home.

Mohammed Abdulkadir Abakir (6)

Mellers Primary School, Nottingham

Elyas' Story

They arrived at the beach.
They rode a big fish and swam under the water.
Then they got off and built a sandcastle.
Then they went home and they were tired so they went to bed and fell asleep.

Elyas Al-Jalam (6)
Mellers Primary School, Nottingham

Oscar's Pirate Story

As the sun rose, Ellie and Spencer could see an island ahead of them. It was called Coconut Peak. As Ellie and Spencer landed on the island Spencer pointed at the skull and crossbones. 'Look!' yelled Spencer.

'What?' said Ellie with a gasp. 'Not those pirates again!'

'Argh! I've found me treasure!' muttered Captain Buttons. 'And what are you doing here?'

'Nothing.'

'Yes nothing!' said Ellie.

'You're coming with me!'

'Where are we going?' said Ellie.

'You're going to walk me plank!'

Spencer gulped.

'What?' said Captain Buttons.

'Whee!' cried Ellie and Spencer, while riding on the dolphins over the sea and waves.

'That was fun,' said Ellie.

'How about a nice, slow, long walk?' said Spencer.

Oscar Daniel Gilliver (7)

Scarcliffe Primary School, Chesterfield

Lewis' Jungle Story

In the deep, dark jungle, there were lots of green bushy leaves and tall jungle vines. It was a beautiful sunny day and Spencer said, 'Time for an adventure!'

Spencer had brown, curly hair and he loved to eat fish and chips. Ellie was a little girl and had blonde hair. She liked spaghetti Bolognese.

Suddenly... they saw a red, terrifying snake. It said, 'Hiss!'

'Eek!' screeched Ellie.

They were both frightened.

'Best go... It's Mr Snake,' said Spencer.

Then they ran and ran until they met a lion. The lion said, 'Do you want to ride on my back?'

'Phew yes please,' said Spencer and Ellie. So they got on and then they were off.

They rode and rode until they got to a lake. The lake was shining brightly.

Finally they were safe. They sneaked back to Ellie's house for tea.

'What an adventure!' said Spencer.

Lewis James Tye (7)
Scarcliffe Primary School, Chesterfield

Ethan's Pirate Story

Ellie and Spencer mysteriously made a boat then paddled to an island with bright, light golden sands.

All of a sudden Ellie and Spencer found a humongous, colossal, gigantic treasure chest. When they saw it they were as happy as if it was Christmas Day.

Then Ellie and Spencer saw a big, fat massive pirate. He shouted, 'Argh! Argh! That's my jewels and money.'

'Oh, we didn't mean to!'

'You have to walk the plank. First you boy, then you next smelly old girl!'

'I'm not a smelly girl.'

'OK, you girl.'

All of a sudden dolphins appeared and Ellie and Spencer rode on them. They rode back to the nice, lovely house.

When they got back... they peacefully relaxed and that day was never ever forgotten as they both had pirate hats.

Ethan Richard Bytheway (7)

Scarcliffe Primary School, Chesterfield

Oliver's Space Story

Ellie and Spencer whooshed up high into space.
'Wow!' said Ellie. 'Look at the twinkling stars.'
'Let's see if we can catch one!' said Spencer.
They didn't know something was watching them.
A little alien called Green had been watching Ellie
and Spencer. Green wanted to play so he beamed
Ellie up into his spaceship.
Then they zoomed off into space and played with
Green's friends. They had lots of fun.
Next there was a fat, scary alien, he was not
friendly and wanted to eat Ellie, Spencer and
Green.
Spencer and Green dropped off Ellie at home
before long and they said
goodbye to her and flew away.

Oliver Raben (6)
Scarcliffe Primary School, Chesterfield

Scarlett's Magical Story

Once upon a time there was an elf and he woke someone up and they went on an adventure. They went the wrong way because they did not know where to go. So they had to do it. They had a pony to ride so they didn't have to walk a long way. Suddenly they met a scary, unhappy dragon, they were as scared as a shy person. They were terrified once they saw it. They stopped straight away.

They stood still for a couple of seconds, then ran as fast as they could away from the scary unhappy dragon.

'Finally, that's over,' said the girl. So they trotted the pony down the hill and they were as happy as if they had a new friend.

But while they were trotting their pony down they found a witch outside of her house made from scrumptious sweets.

She was a nice witch but she wanted their pony so she swapped it for her broom because she wondered if they wanted to fly and they did.

Scarlett Smyth (6)
Scarcliffe Primary School, Chesterfield

Logan's Space Story

Spencer the elf took Ellie to the moon and on the way they saw beautiful stars in space. Earth looked so small.

When they arrived they didn't know that an alien was watching them. The alien also didn't know that Spencer was an elf.

Ellie was picked up by a spaceship. Her bear flew into the air. In a flash, Ellie and her teddy were in the spaceship.

Ellie and the alien flew around space with a flash. Ellie and the alien saw lots of beautiful stars as they went around.

Suddenly Ellie, Spencer, Teddy and the alien saw a disgusting three-eyed monster on the cold floor from the window.

For the rest of the night Ellie went back home and it took Ellie 44 minutes to get to her house. Then she went to sleep.

Logan Andrew Webb (7)
Scarcliffe Primary School, Chesterfield

Katie's Magical Story

In the mysterious, magical forest all of a sudden there was a flash of light and standing gracefully before Ellie and Spencer was Shine, the unicorn. All of a sudden a terrifying dragon popped up out of nowhere and chased Ellie and Spencer away. Spencer and Ellie ran as fast as they possibly could to get away from the scary dragon.
Shine luckily came to the rescue just in time to save them from the dragon.
Suddenly a big scary witch came and asked them what they were doing. They looked really scared. Finally they managed to get home at last. They got back on the witch's wicked broomstick. They were happy again.

Katie Allen (6)

Scarcliffe Primary School, Chesterfield

Isabella's Jungle Story

Ellie was at the jungle and her favourite bit was swinging on the vines. She swung with her teddy and Spencer the elf.

Suddenly she saw a big snake and cuddled Spencer in shock.

Ellie, Spencer and Teddy ran as quickly as they could. They were very frightened.

Then suddenly Ellie saw a lion and cuddled Spencer again but this time she really cuddled him.

But then the lion gave them a smile and Ellie jumped on the lion's back and when her friends got on they rode off.

They got home and Ellie got back into bed. The next minute all her family woke up and said, 'Did you have a good sleep?'

Isabella Hyslop (6)

Scarcliffe Primary School, Chesterfield

Hope's Space Story

Ellie and Spencer were flying in the sky at night-time. They landed on a planet.

They landed on the moon and they didn't know that an alien was watching them.

Suddenly Ellie was flying up into a spaceship but she didn't know. Then she realised she was going into a spaceship and her teddy didn't know either.

Suddenly the girl was flying in the spaceship with a friendly green alien. There were stars.

Suddenly a scary green monster was attacking them.

They landed at the girl's house and she said, 'Thank you.'

Hope Lily-May Webb (6)

Scarcliffe Primary School, Chesterfield

Harry's Space Story

Spencer held Ellie's hand tightly as they travelled into the sky.

After landing on the moon, Spencer put the stars in order of size.

An alien called Zog beamed them up into his spaceship.

Spencer, Ellie and their new alien friends zoomed around the galaxy.

They saw a different alien with lots of eyes and a long tongue. He tried to lick their spaceship.

After a night of fun Zog took Ellie and Spencer home but Spencer decided to stay with Zog as he was having fun.

Harry McEwan (6)

Scarcliffe Primary School, Chesterfield

Joshua's Jungle Story

Ellie, Spencer and Ted arrived at an exotic jungle.
They swung on loopy branches until...
An anaconda stopped them in their tracks!
The anaconda was looking ravenous. He was
staring right at Ted!
Suddenly there was a roar in the jungle. Out leapt
a courageous lion named Frank!
Frank's roar chased the snake away, big time!
Frank took Ellie, Spencer and Ted to some green,
thick vines.
The gang swung safely home ready for the next
adventure.

Joshua Clarke (7)
Scarcliffe Primary School, Chesterfield

Ebony's Zoo Story

Spencer the elf was taking Ellie to the zoo.
They went for a ride on an elephant.
They went to see the panda bears.
They went exploring.
They went to visit the monkeys.
Spencer took Ellie home.

Ebony Jade Cauldewell (6)
Scarcliffe Primary School, Chesterfield

Darcie's Jungle Story

They arrived at the most beautiful jungle ever. Out of the corner of Ellie's eye she saw a bear swinging on a vine. 'Can I have a go?' asked Ellie and Spencer.

'OK,' replied the bear.

'This is fun,' said Ellie.

Soon they came across a snake called Fierce.

'What are you doing?' asked Spencer.

'I'm trying to find something to eat and that is probably you,' laughed Fierce.

In a flash Spencer and Ellie were gone. 'I'm glad we got away in time,' sighed Ellie. 'I've just forgotten, I don't know how to get home,' shouted Ellie. 'Let's keep going. We might even find someone to help and there is a lion.'

'Do you know where I live?' asked Spencer.

'Yes, follow me,' said Lion.

'Hop onto my back and hold on, you're in for a treat,' said Lion.

They whooshed past the bear and the snake then, 'We're home,' declared Ellie.

'Thank you,' said Ellie and Spencer to the lion. Everyone was happy!

Darcie Jones (7)
Shirland Primary School, Alfreton

Lexi's Space Story

They flew to space.

They could see shiny, sparkly stars.

The children picked the stars.

They didn't see the alien watching the kids.

After, the alien picked up Ellie and her teddy.

Ellie was scared of the alien because... the alien was happy.

Spencer the elf was a friend of the alien.

A nasty alien was sticking its tongue out of its mouth.

Ellie went home and she went to bed.

She was happy.

Lexi Wilkinson (5)
Shirland Primary School, Alfreton

Aimee's Magical Story

Once, long ago, there was a girl called Ellie, Spencer the elf, Sparkle the unicorn and Fire the dragon. They went on Sparkle to the fairy house, but they met a dragon on the way. The dragon was crying. They asked him why.

Through his tears the dragon explained why. 'Well, I cannot breathe fire.'

'Oh dragon, we will help you.' So they helped the dragon breathe fire...

The dragon breathed the fire because he was mean so Ellie and Spencer ran away but the dragon followed them but he got lost in the woods. They then went home but on the way they met a witch that was a mean, horrifying witch. The children said, 'Oh witch, witch, can you help?'

The witch gave them a hot chocolate and some lollies because they were so worried. After that the witch said, 'You can have a broom of mine.'

So Spencer and Ellie could go home safe and sound together, happily ever after.

Aimee Louise Hingley (6)

Shirland Primary School, Alfreton

Ellie's Jungle Story

Ellie found a lost bear in the jungle. The baby bear was called Boohoo. Then Spencer the elf said, 'That's a nice name!'

Then an hour later they met a snake called Sneaky the snake. It wanted to... eat the bear but they said, 'You can't eat her.'

They then ran away from the snake and they growled and screamed very loudly. They kept running and running until they got tired.

When they got tired they found a lion. He was kind so they said, 'Can you take us home?'

The lion said, 'Yes, I will take you home.'

On the way home they sang a song for them and the lion to settle down and relax on the way home.

When they got home they went in their house, had a drink and a biscuit and then brushed their teeth and went to bed.

Ellie Grace Hodgetts (7)

Shirland Primary School, Alfreton

Max's Space Story

Once there was a girl sleeping in her bed. Her name was Ellie. She magically disappeared into space. Spencer lived in space, it was his birthday, he had taken Ellie into space.

Ellie and Spencer were counting stars. There was an alien invasion on Mars. Cheek the alien was spying on them.

Ellie got sucked up by a UFO. It was Cheek's UFO. Ellie and Spencer became friends with Cheek. Soon it was time for Ellie to go, so Cheek and Spencer took Ellie home.

Spencer, Ellie and Cheek set off. It was very calm. Ellie said, 'It's amazing.'

Cheek forgot to switch off the sucker, there was a hungry monster. They took the big blobber monster out!

Then Ellie ran home before morning!

Max Jacques (6)
Shirland Primary School, Alfreton

Kara's Zoo Story

Spencer the elf flew Ellie to the zoo. 'Are we going to go on animals?' Ellie said. 'Are we? Are we?' Spencer calmly replied, 'Yes, we are.'

They went on the elephant and they went, 'Wheeeee.' Ellie's bear was on the trunk of the elephant.

They saw pandas. Spencer held a baby panda. Ellie then hugged the mummy panda. She was cuddling Mum.

The elephant walked with Ellie and Spencer. Lots of leaves were around them.

Ellie and her teddy bear saw a monkey eating a banana. Ellie was eating a banana.

Spencer and Ellie went on the elephant home. Spencer got the elephant to the zoo.

Kara Rabbitt (7)
Shirland Primary School, Alfreton

Taelur's Jungle Story

They landed hard in the jungle. They swung fast on three vines.

They then met a slimy snake and the children were scared. The girl was terrified and the boy was petrified.

Then the children were petrified because the snake was scary.

After a while they were in the jungle when they heard a growl... It was a friendly lion and the lion was helpful and massive.

Then the lion said, 'I can take you home.'

'Thanks,' said the children.

One night the children finally returned home. Ellie's mummy was sticking her head out the window and Ellie was happy.

Taelur Brentnall (6)
Shirland Primary School, Alfreton

Lydia's Jungle Story

They landed in the fun jungle with a thump and then they went on the green vines.

They bumped into a snake. The snake was nasty and it played a prank on them.

It was staring at them. They ran away but they were still scared.

When it was later a lion crawled out the bushes and it was a nice lion.

He had seven whiskers and they were smooth...

The lion let the kids go on his back and he ran as fast as he could go.

Finally they got home and they were happy on the green vines and it was night.

Lydia Lightfoot (6)
Shirland Primary School, Alfreton

Jocelyn's Magical Story

They landed in a faraway place near lots of trees. They landed in a tree and they hurt themselves. Suddenly, they found a unicorn lying on some grass. They tried to wake it up but it wouldn't wake up.

Then a fierce dragon came out of an enormous tree. 'Please be kind dragon,' Ellie and Spencer the elf said. The dragon blew out fire then... the unicorn came. They galloped away.

They quickly got off the unicorn and they ran away as fast as lightning. Then they stopped running because it started raining. The rain put the fire out. After a while the unicorn came back and they hopped on the beautiful unicorn and they flew off. They saw lots of lollipops so they stopped so they could eat them.

Suddenly, a cruel witch appeared out of a tree and she took them into her house.

Finally she put one of them in the cage then one of them put the witch in the oven. One of them got the key, unlocked the cage and then they ran away. They went back home.

Jocelyn Trow (6)
Shirland Primary School, Alfreton

Tye's Zoo Story

They landed smoothly in a giant zoo. It was colourful and huge. They saw a helpful elephant who was cute and very ginormous because it was a mummy elephant.

All of a sudden Ellie and Spencer jumped on the huge elephant's back and he ran as fast as a horse. The elephant let Ellie's teddy on his trunk. They saw a giant panda, he had a cute baby panda in his hand. He was very tiny and he couldn't walk yet.

After a bit they got on the elephant's back. Ellie's teddy was wrapped in the elephant's trunk.

The huge, friendly monkey loved bananas, so did Teddy and Ellie. Ellie's tiny teddy was on a big wonky leaf. Ellie's teddy was dangling.

At last they went home. Ellie went home first. Ellie waved to Spencer. Spencer went home and they lived happily ever after.

Tye Holmes (7)
Shirland Primary School, Alfreton

Zachary's Magical Story

They landed in gooey mud and they found a place called the Magic Tree and they met a unicorn. Ellie was shocked because she'd never seen a unicorn before.

Then the elf and Ellie saw the view on a massive hill. They went down the hill and they saw a dragon!

The dragon was faster than Ellie and Elf but they ran like lightning. After a bit they were still running and they tripped over a stone and they flew. 'Argh!' They landed on the unicorn, their hearts pumping like mad. After a bit the elf and Ellie calmed down. Suddenly... a witch was coming. The teddy didn't care, he just ate sweets and chocolate. The witch was mad. She went *pop!*

The elf was so happy he took the broom and flew. Ellie felt safe. Ellie dreamed that Spencer the elf had a good time.

Zachary Tissié (6)

Shirland Primary School, Alfreton

Erin's Zoo Story

They landed in a rough zoo and they looked around. They saw an elephant and it asked if they wanted a ride through the zoo.

They rode the elephant and Ellie was excited because she'd never ridden a big elephant! Soon they passed some bamboo. They heard a loud rattling noise.

Soon they found out it was a panda bear. Ellie liked the panda bear, it was really soft and it was sitting in some bamboo.

They then rode the elephant again. There were lots of leaves and they went through the zoo and the elephant stomped loudly. He carried Teddy.

They saw a monkey. He asked if they wanted a banana. Teddy swung on some vines.

Finally they went home and the elephant and Spencer dropped Ellie off back home. Ellie felt happy because she would get some rest.

Erin Clark (6)

Shirland Primary School, Alfreton

Finley's Zoo Story

They landed with a bump and they saw a big, fat elephant. Ellie and Spencer were excited because the elephant said, 'Get on my back.'

They got on the elephant's back for a ride. They were feeling super duper happy. They really liked riding on the elephant.

Suddenly... they saw a huge fluffy panda cuddling Ellie and Ellie's teddy. Spencer the elf was cuddling the cute, fluffy baby panda.

The elephant kept on walking for a while. The teddy was wrapped round the elephant's trunk. They saw 100 green leaves on the way.

All of a sudden they saw a huge monkey, it was eating a banana. Ellie's teddy slid down a vine like Superman.

Finally they went home. They felt happy. They had a rest when they got home.

Finley Kinnear (7)

Shirland Primary School, Alfreton

Taylor's Zoo Story

They landed safely in a zoo. They saw a huge elephant that squirted water at them!

They then rode on the elephant. It was high. Ellie and Spencer were feeling very happy! After that Ellie let the elephant hold her teddy bear on its trunk.

After a while they found a humongous panda. Ellie gave it a cuddle. Spencer the elf held the panda's cute baby.

Then Ellie and Spencer were going back home. They stopped and Spencer pointed at something. They were very scared!

Just then Ellie saw a monkey. It gave her a banana. Ellie's teddy was sliding down a long leaf.

Finally Ellie went home. She waved at Spencer the elf. Ellie's teddy waved too. Ellie felt happy because she got to have a rest.

Taylor Paige Griffiths Whysall (7)

Shirland Primary School, Alfreton

Kain's Zoo Story

They landed in a bush next to a zoo. It was a bit noisy. They heard leaves rattling in the trees and in the bushes.

When they walked in they saw a massive, enormous elephant! It felt very, very high and it was like they might fall off.

After a while they arrived to a smiley panda. Ellie hugged the silly panda, it was black and white. Just then they got back on the elephant's back. Ellie's teddy was rolled up in the elephant's trunk.

All of a sudden they arrived to a happy monkey and it was eating a banana. Then the teddy was swinging on a branch.

Ellie jumped off the elephant's back and she waved goodbye to Spencer the elf. She felt happy because she was back home.

Kain Smith (7)
Shirland Primary School, Alfreton

Beth's Space Story

Spencer was flying in the air with Ellie. Ellie saw lots of stars in the night sky. Ellie was happy that Spencer had gone into space.

Ellie was collecting stars with Spencer. When Spencer turned around he saw an alien, it was called Two.

Ellie and Spencer got caught in a flying saucer. Ellie was amazed to see the moon from a flying saucer.

She saw thousands of stars in the sky. Then the flying saucer broke, *crash clank!* Who will help them now?

Then Ellie saw a space monster, then the alien came in the flying saucer. 'Get it out of the flying saucer.'

The monster went out of the rocket. Spencer was near Ellie's house. Ellie said goodbye and went to sleep.

Beth (7)
Shirland Primary School, Alfreton

Jude's Jungle Story

They landed softly in a bright jungle with lots of colourful tigers.

All of a sudden they saw a massive snake, its fangs were like knives and it was red and blue. Ellie and Spencer were terrified.

The angry snake was chasing them. The snake tried to get them but they were too fast for the snake.

Suddenly they bumped into a lion, he was a kind lion. He was very friendly because he let them ride on his back.

He let them ride on his back and he jumped through the massive green leaves. They got off the lion to try to get home.

They swung back home. Ellie had a nice time. It was very good. 'I liked it because we got to ride on a lion. I am glad we are home,' said Ellie.

Jude Hunter (6)
Shirland Primary School, Alfreton

Sofia's Jungle Story

They landed in a jungle softly and had a picnic. Suddenly, there was a snake trying to eat the picnic and he did.

Then they saw a nice snake. He didn't bite, he was kind but in the jungle Ellie went camping at night. She forgot to zip the tent up, a nasty snake came in to eat Ellie.

But he didn't get to eat Ellie because she put some food out, but she had no food left.

They then met a lion that was nice. He was smiling at the children. They felt scared of the lion.

After that they had a ride on the lion.

Finally, they swung on vines and went back home.

Sofia Jones (5)
Shirland Primary School, Alfreton

Leland's Zoo Story

They landed softly outside the zoo gates. A cute, smiley elephant was poking his head out of the gates.

When they got on the massive elephant's back across the beautiful zoo they looked at the tall bamboo.

Just then they saw a panda and he was sitting next to some bamboo. Ellie was cuddling him and she saw a cute panda.

After that they got on the elephant's back. They carried on...

Soon they saw a monkey and it had a banana. Teddy was sliding down a leaf.

Finally they got on the elephant but Spencer took the elephant to the zoo.

Leland Shipley (7)
Shirland Primary School, Alfreton

Chloe's Jungle Story

They landed softly in the jungle and swung on spiky green vines. They felt like jumping for joy because the vines were fun!

Then they bumped into a slithery snake and the slithery snake hissed at them. They felt terrified so they ran away!

The slithery snake chased them every day.

Suddenly a lion jumped out of a bush, it was going to eat them! Oh no, they ran away again.

After that they had a ride on the lion and went fast. Finally they got home. Ellie's mummy waved to her.

When they went home she felt happy and she played with her toys.

Chloe Redfern (6)

Shirland Primary School, Alfreton

Thomas' Pirate Story

They landed on an island, then found a boat and the boat was old. They were rowing to another island.

They saw a treasure box and they opened it and there was treasure but Spencer said, 'Look at that pirate!' Ellie looked and she shut the box.

The pirate was angry. He got his sword. 'Keep away!'

All of a sudden the pirate made Spencer and Ellie walk the plank but they didn't want to so the pirate pushed them.

But they jumped on dolphins and the pirate was cross!

They then went home and they were happy!

Thomas Jacob Shaw (6)
Shirland Primary School, Alfreton

Alice's Magical Story

They landed safely in Magical Land very soon and they rode on a cute, friendly, gold, pink and white cuddly unicorn!

They then got chased by a fierce dragon... He blew fire out of his mouth. They ran away!

Ellie tripped over her teddy. She cut herself and she nearly got eaten by a dragon.

Just then, Ellie and Spencer found the unicorn!

They then saw a witch and she locked them in a cage. They got out of the cage. The witch looked again and they were gone.

They went home on a broom and Ellie was happy.

Alice Ellie-Mai Wheatley (6)
Shirland Primary School, Alfreton

Liley's Magical Story

They landed in a magical world and they saw a good unicorn. They got on it for a while.
Ellie was scared of the dragon.
The children were running away from the dragon. They were scared of the dragon.
After that they went on a unicorn. It was fun because the unicorn went softly on the floor.
The weird witch told the children off. They were scared of the witch. 'You can't have my lollipops,' said the wicked witch.
Ellie went back home and she was happy. She played with her toys.

Liley Francis Hill (6)
Shirland Primary School, Alfreton

Evie's Magical Story

They landed softly in a magical land. They met a beautiful unicorn and then Ellie bumped into a dragon.

Then Ellie saw a fierce dragon... The dragon nearly ate Ellie. After a while the dragon chased Ellie.

Spencer and Ellie then saw the fierce dragon. It ran after Ellie and Spencer. Ellie was terrified.

Later Ellie and Spencer got on the same unicorn and they felt happy.

Next they saw a cruel witch. The witch was a nasty, horrid, evil witch.

Ellie flew back home.

Evie Hodgetts (6)

Shirland Primary School, Alfreton

Owen's Magical Story

They landed in a magical place, then they found a unicorn who took them everywhere.

They then saw a fierce dragon and it blew fire, a lot of fire!

Then they started to run away from the fierce dragon!

After a while the unicorn blew by. It landed then they jumped on and flew away.

Suddenly they saw a sweet garden. They started to pick sweets and lollipops.

Soon they flew like lightning on a broom. They returned home. She felt safe and happy.

Owen Harris (6)
Shirland Primary School, Alfreton

Bella's Space Story

They met an alien and the alien took them to his glowing, colourful ship.

Then Ellie and her friend went into the alien's ship.

Suddenly they saw a meaner and bigger alien come to try and eat Ellie and Spencer. They ran away.

Ellie and Spencer had a little ride in the ship.

Then the meaner and bigger alien came again but just in time they jumped into the alien's ship.

Finally Ellie went home and she went back to bed.

Bella Meeks (5)
Shirland Primary School, Alfreton

Isabelle's Magical Story

They landed in a soft magical place with a magical unicorn and it looked beautiful.

After then a fierce dragon was going to eat Ellie, then Ellie ran away from the dragon.

Then Ellie saw the dragon, the dragon chased Ellie. They were scared of the dragon.

After a while they saw a unicorn and they rode on the unicorn.

Then a witch came and the witch nearly got Ellie.

They then got the broom and they went home.

They felt happy.

Isabelle Glover (6)

Shirland Primary School, Alfreton

Harry's Jungle Story

They landed in a jungle safely and they jumped on some long vines.

Then they ran into a scaly, big, long, hissing snake and it tried to hypnotise them!

But then the spell broke and they ran away as fast as a cheetah.

They then met a lion and they asked if they could ride on his back.

But then they rode home and the lion stopped and they got off.

They rode home and they felt safe.

Harry Jones (6)
Shirland Primary School, Alfreton

Charlotte's Magical Story

First they travelled to a magic place. They travelled on a unicorn. They were happy and petrified. They landed terribly because there were bumps everywhere. There was a stomping noise. They thought it was a dragon! They ran away.

Then the dragon smelt them and the dragon found something and they ran outside! They found a tree so they hid next to the tree and they found their pals.

The elf was called Spencer. The dragon followed Spencer. Suddenly, they found the unicorn. It was nice to Spencer.

They walked in the woods. They found a nice little cottage. It was made out of cookies and sweets. They ate the house. They had tummy ache. A witch came. She saw them. She put them in a cage and they were scared. They escaped and the unicorn took them home. They went into the bathroom to brush their teeth. They put their PJs on and went to bed.

Charlotte Richards (6)

Shirland Primary School, Alfreton

Layla-Jean's Zoo Story

Ellie and Spencer went to the zoo. They were excited and they wanted to buy something but they couldn't because other people needed to see it.

And then they went on the elephant and it was fun and he was holding a panda and they had fun.

They met the panda, she had some babies too and Ellie hugged her and Spencer had a baby panda, she was super fluffy.

Next they went on an elephant, he had his trunk wrapped around a panda but it did not hurt.

And then they met a monkey, he had a giant banana and Ellie had a banana too.

Then they went home. 'Goodbye.'

'Are we going home?'

'Yes.'

'OK bye, see you another day.'

Layla-Jean Perry (6)
St George's Primary School, Swadlincote

Olivia's Jungle Story

Ellie and Spencer swung on enormous vines. They went swinging and they could hear swishing leaves and tweeting birds when they were swinging vine to vine to vine.

They saw a terrifying snake. It was yellow and a lovely green colour.

They ran away from the yellow and bluey-green snake. They could hear sticks breaking. 'Run, there is a terrifying snake!'

There was a roaring lion and swaying leaves.

'What are you going to give me, a ride?' asked Ellie 'I'll give you a ride, what's your name?' asked the lion.

'My name is Ellie. Thank you for the ride.'

'It was a pleasure.'

They swung back home.

Olivia Grace McDermott (6)

St George's Primary School, Swadlincote

Corey's Pirate Story

Ellie and Spencer were rowing a boat and the waves were waving. Next the boat glided through the waves.

Also they landed on an island and they saw a treasure chest. Also it was overflowing.

After that they saw Captain Blackbird. 'Who are you?' said Captain Blackbird.

'We are Ellie and Spencer,' they said.

Next they walked the plank and Ellie was shocked. Also Captain Blackbird said, 'Yo ho, ho, ho!'

Also they rowed on the dolphin back home. Also they were happy again.

Spencer and Ellie were very happy and excited and it was night-time.

Corey Harrison-Ross (6)

St George's Primary School, Swadlincote

Cameron's Pirate Story

Spencer was rowing on a brown boat with a little girl named Ellie. The sun was shining down on them. There were palm trees, a bright sun, a boat and wavy sea. The sea is very blue and very wavy and it is very blue.

Finally they arrived at the island. They saw a treasure chest, it was full of shining gold. Also there were palm trees and an island full of playful sand. Spencer and Ellie did not play with the sand though.

All of a sudden a pirate saw Spencer and Ellie open the treasure chest. The pirate was very angry with them because they opened the chest.

The escape plan was to walk the plank so they did that. Both of them walked the plank. The pirate was angry, he did not want them to walk the plank.

They escaped on a dolphin, they did not expect that the dolphins would pick them up.

They arrived at their house. Ellie was very happy to be back home with her family again. She was very happy.

Cameron Thompson (6)
St George's Primary School, Swadlincote

Max's Pirate Story

Ellie and Spencer rowed a boat across the blue sea. As they went they could hear trees swaying in the breeze and they could see the shining sun, it was bright!

Ellie found a brown treasure chest and even her teddy had a crown on. It was amazing, excellent and it was fantastic.

Suddenly a mean pirate showed up, he was angry. He thought they were stealing his treasure. He said, 'Grrr!' swinging his sword!

Next, the pirate made Spencer walk the plank. He was scared, he thought he would be eaten by a shark.

After they landed in the water they took a ride on a dolphin, it was fun until they arrived on land and walked and walked.

They were so tired they didn't even notice they were nearly home.

Max Evans (6)

St George's Primary School, Swadlincote

Wiktoria's Zoo Story

Ellie and Spencer finally arrived at the colourful zoo. Ellie just saw a massive elephant's trunk. She was excited just like the sun. There were some elephants and giraffes.

Next Ellie had a ride on an enormous elephant! A teddy bear was on his trunk. Ellie had a ride near the trees.

Then Ellie saw a fat panda. Ellie cuddled the panda and Spencer was holding a baby panda.

Ellie had a ride again and the teddy was on the trunk. Spencer had a great ride too. They enjoyed the great ride so much!

The teddy got off the trunk. The monkey was eating a banana and Ellie was too. The bananas were yellow.

Finally Ellie needed to go home. Spencer waved at Ellie on the elephant.

Wiktoria Laskauska (6)

St George's Primary School, Swadlincote

Oliver's Pirate Story

When Ellie and Spencer got on the brown boat they saw a palm tree, bright sun and a green bush. They got to an island and they found treasure. Also pirates were following them and Spencer pointed. 'Eek, I'm worried.'

The pirate's name was Jack Sparrow and he was angry with them for stealing the treasure. Also Ellie's teddy was on Spencer's leg.

Spencer is walking the plank because he stole the treasure. Ellie is nervous about Spencer walking the plank!

Ellie and Spencer are riding dolphins back home. Also they are happy going on a dolphin's back home.

It is night-time and they are home. Spencer is holding Ellie's hand back.

Oliver Clarke (6)

St George's Primary School, Swadlincote

Oliver's Zoo Story

At last they made it to the zoo! There was a colourful sign. Ellie and Spencer were just outside the zoo.

They rode on an elephant and the elephant caught a monkey with his trunk. There were tall trees almost everywhere.

Ellie hugged a panda and Spencer hugged a baby panda. There were lots of tall trees behind the panda.

They rode again on an elephant but this time there were gigantic leaves. The elephant was as tall as a skyscraper.

They met a gorilla and had a banana each. There was a monkey swinging very fast.

They rode on an elephant one more time home and they waved goodbye to each other.

Oliver Whiten (6)

St George's Primary School, Swadlincote

Amelia-Rose's Zoo Story

Ellie and Spencer were going to the zoo.
Ellie brought her teddy bear with her so it could keep her happy.
As they went on they got a ride on an elephant.
Also they saw gigantic trees and they saw big leaves.
Next they went to the pandas. There were little pandas and big pandas. Ellie hugged the panda and she smiled at Spencer.
After that they got another ride on an elephant. Spencer nearly got hit by a leaf.
They went to see the monkeys and Ellie had a banana to eat and she liked the monkeys.
At last Ellie got home and Spencer dropped her off. And it was nearly bedtime.

Amelia-Rose Bevington (6)
St George's Primary School, Swadlincote

Madison's Zoo Story

Ellie and Spencer arrived at the noisy zoo. They saw an elephant's trunk and a giraffe's head.

They were riding on a gigantic elephant. They saw some bamboo. There was a baby panda on the elephant's trunk.

They met a mummy panda with some cute baby pandas. Ellie hugged the mummy panda. Spencer was holding a baby panda.

They went through a bunch of itchy leaves. A baby panda was on the elephant's trunk.

Ellie saw a gigantic monkey holding a big banana. Ellie had a small banana.

They had a long day, it was time to go home.

Madison Rylee Mae (6)

St George's Primary School, Swadlincote

Daisy's Zoo Story

After a long fly they got to the zoo and Ellie saw an elephant and a giraffe peeking out of the gate.

Next they went on a bumpy elephant ride. Ellie's teddy had a ride on the elephant's trunk.

Next Ellie and Spencer went to see the pandas and Ellie cuddled the panda.

After that they had another ride on the elephant.

Then they saw a monkey and Ellie and the monkey had a banana.

After a busy day Ellie went home but before she said, 'Goodbye.' They all lived happily ever after.

Daisy Wilson (6)

St George's Primary School, Swadlincote

Maria's Zoo Story

Ellie was so excited. She could see elephants and tall giraffes.

Spencer and Ellie had a ride on an elephant and they could see everything.

She cuddled a panda and he cuddled her toy. Also Spencer held his baby.

After that they had another ride on the elephant before they went to see the cheeky monkeys.

'Wow,' said Ellie, 'a monkey.' Ellie asked if she could have a banana and he said yes!

It was time for Ellie to go home but she had a very fun time at the zoo.

Maria Louise McGinty (6)
St George's Primary School, Swadlincote

Henry's Zoo Story

Spencer and Ellie were excited to go to the zoo.
They saw an elephant and a giraffe.
They went on a gigantic elephant and the bear
went on his trunk, it was fun.
Spencer and Ellie arrived at the pandas. Ellie
hugged the big panda and Spencer held the little
baby panda.
They rode on the elephant again and the bear was
picked up this time.
The monkey was eating a banana. He shared it
with Ellie and the bear swung on a rope.
Ellie went home and Spencer waved bye-bye.

Henry Howlett (6)

St George's Primary School, Swadlincote

Zoe's Zoo Story

Ellie and Spencer arrived at the zoo. There was a cheeky elephant and a giraffe.
Ellie and Spencer went on an adventure and they could hear different sounds.
Spencer and Ellie got off the elephant. Ellie was having a cuddle with a panda.
They were as high as a mountain and the elephant had Ellie's teddy.
Then Ellie was having a little snack and it was a banana. Ellie's teddy was swinging on a vine.
Then Ellie went home to go back to sleep in her own bed.

Zoe Topliss (6)
St George's Primary School, Swadlincote

Thomas' Pirate Story

Ellie and Spencer sailed on a brown boat. Also they sailed in the slow, wavy sea.

Wow! There was a treasure chest and Ellie stood on top of it. Spencer shouted, 'Get down, there's a ship.'

A pirate came out of the ship and he said, 'Hey, that's my treasure.'

The pirate made them walk the plank. Spencer walked the plank first.

It was lucky dolphins were there. The dolphins were friendly.

They went home and lived happily ever after.

Thomas Hadley (6)
St George's Primary School, Swadlincote

Neve's Zoo Story

They got to the zoo. Ellie and Spencer were excited. They saw an elephant peeking out of the zoo.

Next they took a ride on the elephant, a baby panda was on its trunk.

Spencer was holding a really cute panda. Ellie gave the mummy a hug.

Then they had another ride on the elephant, a leaf hit Spencer's head, 'Ouch!'

Then they met a huge monkey. He was eating a banana.

Then it was time to go home.

Neve Edwards (6)
St George's Primary School, Swadlincote

Emilia-Rose's Zoo Story

Ellie and Spencer saw a sign that said: 'Zoo'. They could see a giraffe and an elephant.

They rode on the elephant. On his grey trunk was a bear.

Soon they got to the pandas! They were so cute and soft.

After that they went through the wavy leaves.

The monkey was eating a yellow banana. He is a silly billy.

Spencer waved goodbye. Goodnight.

Emilia-Rose Ward (6)

St George's Primary School, Swadlincote

Ronon's Pirate Story

Spencer and Ellie were in the little brown boat.
They found the pirate's treasure.
The pirate was cross with them for finding his treasure.
They walked the plank to go for a swim.
The dolphins took them for a ride.
Ellie and Spencer went back home.

Ronon Connor Smith (7)
St George's Primary School, Swadlincote

Ashton's Zoo Story

Ellie and Spencer were excited because they'd arrived.
They rode on an elephant uphill in the sun.
Ellie cuddled the soft panda.
The elephant stomped and stomped.
The monkey was eating a banana.
Ellie got home on an elephant.

Ashton Dooner (6)
St George's Primary School, Swadlincote

Jamie's Zoo Story

Ellie and Spencer arrived at the zoo. They were happy and noisy. Ellie took her teddy.
They went on an elephant for a walk through the zoo.
They stopped next to pandas. They hugged the pandas.
The next stop was a monkey and they ate some bananas.
They went home, one went on an elephant and one walked.

Jamie Scott (6)
St George's Primary School, Swadlincote

Ethan's Zoo Story

They travelled to a zoo. Apparently it was empty! Ellie and Spencer saw an elephant at the gate! It was huge and kind.

The elephant, Ellie and Spencer travelled freely through the zoo. 'This is so fun,' said Ellie and Spencer smiled.

First they met a panda and a baby panda. 'I love this panda!' said Ellie. The two pandas smiled. Also they were fluffy and cute.

Elephant said, 'Last animal.'

'Is it a tiger?' said the girl.

'No,' said the elephant.

'Gorilla?'

'Yes.'

Then they did meet a gorilla, he shared a banana. Ellie loves bananas and Teddy was on a vine.

'Time to go home, bye,' said Spencer to Ellie.

'Bye,' Ellie said.

Ethan Allsobrook (7)

St John's CE Primary School, Ripley

Riniya's Zoo Story

Ellie and Spencer went to the biggest zoo in the world and that zoo was on Fletcher Street and the code was DE5 3BD.

Then Spencer and Ellie found a nice, friendly and grey elephant that let Spencer and Ellie ride on his back. Did you know that elephants weigh over 50kg?

Ellie and Spencer met a kind, helpful panda and a cute, little panda in Spencer's hand.

Then they rode back on the nice, friendly and grey elephant and headed to the next funny animal.

The next funny animal was a big gorilla that was eating a white, yummy banana and he gave a banana to Ellie.

Then they went back on the elephant and he took Spencer and Ellie back home so they didn't have to do any more exploring.

Riniya Lawrence (7)
St John's CE Primary School, Ripley

Noemi's Space Story

They didn't only fly over the rooftops but off to space. They flew to burning Mars.

When they got there they started to pick big and small stars. But they hadn't noticed the alien...

The alien had gone to his ship and sucked them up. When they got in the ship the alien said, 'My name is Slod.'

Slod said, 'Would you like a tour around space?'

Ellie and Spencer said, 'Yes of course.' So they went around till they got to the moon.

They saw a scary monster with a long tongue. Ellie wanted to go home. So she shouted. So they went home quickly.

Ellie was very glad indeed. So everyone said goodbye to each other. Ellie ran into her bedroom.

Noemi Skocna (7)
St John's CE Primary School, Ripley

Aaron's Jungle Story

One night Ellie was woken up by Spencer and he said, 'Shall we go on an adventure?'

They went to the jungle. When they got there they swung on some vines.

But they bumped into a snake. The snake was a nasty little thing and the snake chased them.

When the snake was chasing them they bumped into a big, nice lion.

The lion said, 'Do you want to jump onto my back, I'll take you home.'

The lion is so fast, thought Ellie. When the lion stopped he said, 'Call me when you need a lift.'

Before they knew it they were home and Ellie went back to sleep because it had been a good day.

Aaron Newham (7)

St John's CE Primary School, Ripley

Josh's Jungle Story

Spencer and Ellie and their teddy were swinging on some vines in the jungle. The vines were wrapped around the tree so they could swing on them.

When they had got down they met a long stripy snake. Ellie and Spencer were scared.

The snake said, 'I want to eat you!'

Ellie and Spencer ran away because they were scared.

Then they met a lion, the lion was smiling a bit so Ellie and Spencer were puzzled if it was friendly or not.

The lion was friendly so they went on its back. They liked it.

They found some other vines and they swung back home. They lived happily ever after.

Josh Andrews (7)
St John's CE Primary School, Ripley

William's Magical Story

They flew to a magical world. They found a unicorn called Rainbow who was rainbow-coloured. Suddenly there was a savage roar and a dragon appeared.

He hated humans and elves. Spencer and Ellie ran and ran and ran! Then they found Rainbow. 'Run, Rainbow, run!' yelled Spencer.

Rainbow ran. They ran for miles and miles. Eventually they found a nice witch.

She found some lollies for them. Then they borrowed her broomstick. Spencer promised to bring it back.

They landed at Ellie's house. 'Bye!' said Ellie.

'Bye!' said Spencer.

William Moulding (7)
St John's CE Primary School, Ripley

Grace's Magical Story

When they jumped over the rooftops they saw an island no one was on. They landed on the unicorn. Then they saw a dragon. The dragon was evil so it breathed fire.

They ran away. Why they were running away was because the dragon got mad.

Then they got back on the unicorn. The unicorn flew to the witch.

The witch said, 'Do you want a lollipop?'

They said, 'Yes please.'

And they went on the broom and they went back home.

Grace Dobson (7)

St John's CE Primary School, Ripley

Alexa's Magical Story

Ellie and Spencer ended up on a pink unicorn with blue eyes and white horns and shiny teeth. Ellie and Spencer jumped on the unicorn.

The unicorn stopped because Olivia ran out of breath and they met a mean red dragon with red eyes and red and orange fire.

Ellie and Spencer ran away from the dragon. Spencer talked to Ellie and said, 'What a mean, horrifying dragon.'

Ellie and Spencer found Olivia in a fancy field and she flew away to her family but they found a witch. They asked the witch for some food and she magicked some doughnuts and some chocolate biscuits.

Spencer borrowed a broomstick and flew away to Ellie's house and Ellie said, 'Thank you.'

Alexa Jane Beighton (7)

St John's CE Primary School, Ripley

Leah's Space Story

Spencer picked up Ellie and they went to space and they arrived in space.

But an alien was behind them. Spencer got some stars, he was getting stars for Ellie too.

The alien took Ellie and Teddy. She flew into the spaceship and Spencer was hiding in the back and Spencer saw the monster.

The alien waved and Ellie waved to the other aliens and a shooting star came past them.

They saw a monster with three eyes and a long tongue and lots of legs and sharp teeth. Ellie was scared.

Ellie went home. Spencer said bye and the alien said goodbye.

Leah May Leivers (7)

St John's CE Primary School, Ripley

Mitchell's Space Story

Ellie was in bed. She heard a knocking at her window. It was Spencer and Spencer said, 'Come and have an adventure with me.'
They set off and they landed on the moon, and on the moon was a friendly alien and it was staring at them.
The alien lifted Teddy and Ellie into his flying saucer.
They set off and they flew and flew and flew until they saw a monster in the distance.
The monster had three legs and a ten metre tongue.
Then the alien took them home. The alien said, 'Thank you for meeting me. You are my friend.'

Mitchell Gillott (6)

St John's CE Primary School, Ripley

Olivia's Space Story

They had flown up to space and it was very, very, very high and dark too.

But while they were catching stars there was an alien behind them who was being noisy.

Then the alien grabbed his spaceship and sucked them up in his spaceship, even Teddy got sucked up.

Then they went for a look around space and they saw lots and lots of massive stars.

But then they saw a massive monster that licked the spaceship and then it nearly licked them up.

So they went and dropped Ellie off at her house and Teddy of course because they were tired.

Olivia Shaw (6)

St John's CE Primary School, Ripley

Sam's Space Story

At the desert island it was a colourful desert island. They found palm trees and found lots of treasure on the island.

Spencer and Ellie found lots and lots of treasure but then a boat appeared.

A pirate had a sword, he was wearing colourful clothes with a rainbow-coloured parrot and a rainbow-coloured coat.

He made Spencer the elf walk the plank.

Ellie walked the plank after Spencer. Ellie was so scared.

The dolphins saved Spencer, Ellie and also the teddy bear.

They found pirate hats in the treasure chest and went home.

Sam Priest (7)
St John's CE Primary School, Ripley

Marrie Chloe's Magical Story

When they arrived they had a ride on a unicorn on the magical path.

Then, when they got off the unicorn, they saw a fierce fire-breathing dragon with hot fire, sharp teeth, big scales and long claws.

Then the dragon was chasing them. The dragon was so fast that it was breathing fire to stop them.

Then they hopped on the magical unicorn and went to the witch's house.

They saw a witch then they tricked her with one of her spells and got her broom.

They got home on the witch's magical broom.

Marrie Chloe Medina (7)
St John's CE Primary School, Ripley

Imogen's Magical Story

Spencer and Ellie woke up and they had a ride on the unicorn with Teddy.

Then they saw a terrifying dragon that blew fire, had sharp claws and angry eyes.

And then Ellie and Spencer and Teddy ran away from the dragon.

And then they got back on the unicorn with Teddy Bear and galloped along.

Then they saw a witch and she gave them a lollipop but they were poisoned.

Then they went back home on the broom and on the broom they zoomed back home and Teddy was on the edge of the broom.

Imogen Smith (7)

St John's CE Primary School, Ripley

Anthony's Space Story

They went on a unicorn called Emily, she flew them but a stone fell in their way.

Then they came across a dragon, he had teeth, spikes and claws.

Then Ellie and Spencer ran as fast as they could. Then they hid behind some trees.

Then the unicorn took them to a gingerbread house, but who lived there?

A witch lived there. She had some lollipops. She said, 'I'll get you home. Take my broom,' said the witch.

'Thank you,' said Ellie, and home they went.

Anthony Edward Sedgwick (7)

St John's CE Primary School, Ripley

Olivia's Pirate Story

They rowed to a tropical island with palm trees. There were lots of people, some came on boats and some didn't.

Then they found some treasure in the sand but then a pirate came on a ship with huge sails and a huge flag.

Then they met a pirate with a black beard and a sword. It was his treasure!

He forced them to walk the plank. So they did but then something magical happened.

Dolphins came to rescue them so they rode on their backs.

They then lived happily ever after.

Olivia Ellen Steele (7)
St John's CE Primary School, Ripley

Asante's Pirate Story

Ellie and Spencer arrived in a boat and Ellie and Spencer saw something in the distance.

It was a treasure chest but Spencer saw a pirate ship in the distance and Captain Hook was coming their way! He thought that Ellie and Spencer were stealing his treasure chest.

So Captain Hook caught Ellie and Spencer.

Captain Hook told them off and he put hats on them and pushed them off the plank.

But luckily dolphins saved Ellie and Spencer.

Then Spencer flew home with Ellie.

Asante Lewis Dzvene (7)
St John's CE Primary School, Ripley

Libby's Magical Story

A unicorn came and Ellie and Spencer rode on the unicorn. They were happy and joyful.

They saw a dragon but Ellie and Spencer were scared and terrified.

So they ran away. Ellie and Spencer ran very fast.

They met the unicorn again and they were happy again and they felt safer with the unicorn.

Then they met a witch. She was being nasty so they snatched her broomstick off her.

They rode on the broomstick back home, Spencer took Ellie back home.

Libby Swanwick (7)

St John's CE Primary School, Ripley

Dexter's Magical Story

They soon arrived at a magical land. They rode on a magical unicorn.

They met a fierce, fire-breathing dragon. It tried to set Ellie and Spencer on fire.

They ran from the fire-breathing dragon in panic.

They got back on the magical unicorn. Ellie and Spencer saw a wooden cottage and went inside. They met a nice witch. The witch let Ellie and Spencer borrow a flying broomstick.

Ellie and Spencer flew back home on the flying broomstick.

Dexter Wells (7)

St John's CE Primary School, Ripley

Chloe's Magical Story

First they met a unicorn. They rode the unicorn as fast as they could across the trees. Ellie, Spencer, the teddy and the unicorn were fast.
They met a dragon, he was fierce. He was mean. He had red eyes and yellow and black teeth. The dragon could blow out fire.
The dragon was blowing out fire.
They found the unicorn again. They rode it across the trees over the birds.
They met a wicked witch.
They stole her broomstick and flew home.

Chloe Lea Cole (7)
St John's CE Primary School, Ripley

Leah's Space Story

Ellie and Spencer flew up to space and they saw yellow glowing stars.

They landed on the moon and Spencer started catching stars. There was an alien being nasty.

Then the alien sucked Ellie and Spencer up into his ship.

Then they took off and he wanted to be their friend, he took Ellie back home.

When they were taking Ellie home they saw a monster with a long tongue.

They finally got back at Ellie's home and everyone said goodbye.

Leah Parkin (7)

St John's CE Primary School, Ripley

Riley's Magical Story

Ellie heard a unicorn and they went to see the unicorn's family.

On the way they heard a noise and it was an evil dragon. He was red and his eyes were angry.

They ran away because the dragon was trying to eat them.

They found the unicorn. They travelled a bit more.

They heard another noise and it was a witch, she was a nice witch and she magicked some food.

After that the witch gave them the broom and they went back home.

Riley Williams (7)

St John's CE Primary School, Ripley

Sophie-Paige's Magical Story

Ellie got a unicorn from a magic field and got on the unicorn. Spencer got onto the unicorn as well, it was called Dan.

They found a dragon. He was a nasty dragon. He was hungry and he breathed fire and he was a red dragon.

The dragon was chasing Ellie and Spencer.

They got back to the unicorn and they were hungry.

Then they saw a witch. Ellie said she and Spencer would try a lolly then they went home.

Sophie-Paige Walshaw

St John's CE Primary School, Ripley

Porshia's Zoo Story

One night Ellie and Spencer went to the zoo and when they got there there was an elephant peeking out.

The elephant let the children sit on his back.

They met a panda and its baby panda too.

The elephant took the children to the chimp who was eating a banana and Ellie was eating a banana too.

Then Ellie went home and waved to Spencer.

Porshia Boot (7)
St John's CE Primary School, Ripley

Isabel's Magical Story

Ellie and Spencer the elf went on a unicorn. It was magical and fun. The name of the unicorn was Emily.

They flew off Emily the unicorn and they flew into the dragon's cage and the girl was scared of the dragon.

Ellie, the teddy and Spencer the elf ran and they were all scared of the dragon.

Emily the unicorn came back to save them from the big dragon.

Ellie, Teddy and Spencer the elf walked into a nice witch. She gave Teddy a lollipop. Teddy said it was yummy.

The witch gave them her broom to fly home. 'That was great,' said Spencer the elf.

Ellie was cold, Teddy said, 'Wow, what an adventure!'

Isabel Sophie Dickson (6)
St Mary's RC Primary School, Glossop

Melissa's Jungle Story

Spencer, Ellie and Teddy were swinging on big vines. They were swinging through huge trees in the jungle.

They met a friendly snake. Spencer and Ellie were scared of the snake even though he said he was friendly.

Spencer, Ellie and Teddy were running away from the snake because it stuck its tongue out and tried to eat them.

They met a lion. It looked happy. Spencer, Ellie and Teddy were not sure whether he was friendly.

The lion was friendly and took Spencer, Ellie and Teddy for a ride on his back and they enjoyed it.

Spencer took Teddy and Ellie home and they had a swing on some vines on their way.

Melissa Crutchley (6)
St Mary's RC Primary School, Glossop

Molly's Jungle Story

Ellie and Spencer went to the jungle with lots of cute and scary animals. They went onto some giant vines.

Suddenly they saw a fierce snake looking at them. 'Stand back Spencer!' shouted Elllie.

The fierce snake chased Spencer and Ellie. But then they got lost in the jungle.

Then they saw a nice lion near some lovely looking bushes.

Then he let Spencer and Ellie ride on his back. 'This is a fun ride,' said Ellie happily.

Then Spencer and Ellie went back onto the vines and went back home. When Ellie got home she went back into her cosy bed and went to sleep.

Molly Jessica Buller (6)
St Mary's RC Primary School, Glossop

Scarlet's Magical Story

They arrived at Elfland. It looked fun and they went on a unicorn, it was also fun.

While they were riding on her she smelt a dragon. She tripped and they fell off. When they saw the dragon they ran.

They ran as fast as they could. 'Thanks, you helped me Spencer, you're my hero!' said Ellie.

Then they saw the unicorn so they got on her back. They rode until they stopped. They saw a witch.

The witch looked creepy. So they ran away. But she was a nice witch. They hugged.

Then they flew off into the sky. They said goodbye.

Scarlet Findlay (6)
St Mary's RC Primary School, Glossop

Alexi's Zoo Story

Ellie and Spencer found a zoo. Emily the elephant and Grizzly the giraffe welcomed them at the gate. Emily took them around the zoo where they found a very scared baby panda who was lost.

They picked up the baby panda and took him home to his daddy. Daddy Panda gave Ellie a big hug.

They found a shop of bananas. They bought ten. They all had some and saved the rest.

Then they met a monkey. They gave him the rest of the bananas.

After the bananas Emily took them home.

Alexi Bray (6)
St Mary's RC Primary School, Glossop

Ethan's Magical Story

They went to an ancient forest that had dragons, unicorns and witches.

Then they saw a dragon and nearly got burned. The dragon had his shiny claws up and was breathing red fire.

Then they ran away from the dragon doing the same thing.

After, they went on a unicorn and rode to a witch.

When they arrived at the witch, the witch shouted, 'Take those lollipops!'

Finally they flew back to the red cottage on a broomstick.

Ethan Liang (7)

St Mary's RC Primary School, Glossop

Layla's Zoo Story

They went to the zoo. They saw an elephant.
They rode an elephant. They said, 'That was lots of fun.'
Then they saw a panda. He was cuddly.
They climbed back on the elephant.
He took them to see the monkeys. They ate bananas with the monkeys.
Ellie said, 'It is time to go home.' So she said bye to the elf. Ellie said, 'I will miss you.'

Layla Flanagan (6)

St Mary's RC Primary School, Glossop

Elliott's Magical Story

They went to a magical forest.

They saw a fire-breathing dragon.

They ran away.

They got on the unicorn.

They met a witch.

They got on the broomstick and flew home.

Elliott Hanks (5)

St Mary's RC Primary School, Glossop

Kacie's Space Story

Someone knocked on the window. Ellie was scared so she ran into her mum's room. Mum said, 'Go back in your room.'
Ellie heard the noise again. She looked out of her window and she went somewhere.
When they got to space they were surprised because they saw 100 stars and they wanted to pick them all.
Ellie heard a noise again. An alien shouted for Ellie to go into the spaceship. The alien put the light on and they were going up into the spaceship.
Ellie wasn't scared and she said, 'Bye-bye, see you again soon.'
In the spaceship they saw a monster that was very big and they turned their lights on again and it was going up.
The alien was going out of space to drop Ellie off at her house.

Kacie Barker (6)
The Bramble Academy, Mansfield

Lacey's Magical Story

When Ellie and Spencer arrived they found themselves in a magical land. Just then Ellie and Spencer saw a strange kind of dark black cloud so they went to see what it was.

Just as they arrived at the dark cloud of smoke they realised it was a huge, ferocious fire-breathing dragon. Suddenly the dragon tried to set fire to all three of them.

The dragon began to chase them until they found their unicorn. 'Phew!' said Ellie.

Ellie and Spencer got on the magical unicorn and flew off into the sky.

Just as they got off the unicorn they saw an ugly, creepy witch but they took her broom.

When they took her broom they flew home.

Lacey Louise Churchill (7)

The Bramble Academy, Mansfield

Jorja's Magical Story

Ellie and the unicorn were in Magic World. The unicorn was kind. She had a pink mane and tail. The sun shone in the sky.

When they got to the top of the mountain, a fierce dragon was breathing fire out of his mouth. They ran away. Spencer and Ellie ran away together. The dragon breathed ginormous fire. Ellie and Spencer ran away as fast as they could, so did the teddy bear.

The unicorn rescued them. She galloped away and she took them to the witch.

The witch said, 'I will give you the broom.'

The broom took them home for bedtime. 'Thank you,' said Spencer. The broom was gone.

Jorja Argyle (6)
The Bramble Academy, Mansfield

Logan's Space Story

Spencer took her to outer space past the stars and Earth. Ellie had never been to space before.
Spencer and Ellie picked some stars, then minutes later they got carried away but they didn't notice an alien was onboard.
After that Ellie didn't notice that an alien was about to suck her up with some wavy tentacles. Ellie asked the alien's name. 'My name is Logan.' The alien knew how to fly a spaceship.
Spencer found Ellie with Logan the alien. He put Logan in charge. He sucked up a huge monster. When they landed Ellie said goodbye to Spencer and Logan.

Logan Bridgford (6)
The Bramble Academy, Mansfield

Karta's Space Story

They went up to space. 'Wow!' said Ellie. Ellie brought her teddy along with her. They could see lots of stars in space.

Spencer the elf grabbed a lot of stars. They were standing on the moon. A Martian was sucking them up.

The Martian got his flying saucer. He picked up Spencer the elf, Ellie and her teddy. They got lifted up.

The Martian showed the two around space in his flying saucer. She loved it and it looked really pretty.

There was a big monster. It had a massive tongue. The three of them were scared and the teddy too. The Martian took her home.

Karta Riley Walker-Morgan (7)

The Bramble Academy, Mansfield

Tye's Space Story

Ellie was flying with the elf and then they arrived.
An alien crept up on them but where did they go to?
The alien put up the lever and Ellie came up to space.
They were in space and she had a ride.
They said goodbye to Ellie who said, 'Thank you for having me.'

Tye Boulton (6)

The Bramble Academy, Mansfield

The Storyboards

Here are the fun storyboards
children could choose from...

MAGICAL ADVENTURE

JUNGLE TALE

PIRATE ADVENTURE

SPACE STORY

ZOO ADVENTURE

First published in Great Britain in 2017 by:

YoungWriters

Coltsfoot Drive
Peterborough
PE2 9BF
Telephone: 01733 890066
Website: www.youngwriters.co.uk

Young Writers
Information

We hope you have enjoyed reading this book and that you will continue to in the coming years.

If you're a young writer who enjoys reading and creative writing, or the parent of an enthusiastic poet or story writer, do visit our website **www.youngwriters.co.uk**. Here you will find free competitions, workshops and games, as well as recommended reads, a poetry glossary and our blog.

If you would like to order further copies of this book, or any of our other titles give us a call or visit **www.youngwriters.co.uk**.

Young Writers
Remus House
Coltsfoot Drive
Peterborough
PE2 9BF

(01733) 890066
info@youngwriters.co.uk